NINE RULES OF
ENGAGEMENT

JEANNETTE WINTERS

Jeannette Winters
Author Contact

website:
JeannetteWinters.com
email:
authorjeannettewinters@gmail.com
Facebook:
Author Jeannette Winters
Twitter:
JWintersAuthor
Newsletter Signup:
www.jeannettewinters.com/newsletter

Also follow me on:
BookBub:
bookbub.com/authors/jeannette-winters
Goodreads:
https://www.goodreads.com/author/show/
13514560.Jeannette_Winters
Pinterest:
https://www.pinterest.com/authorjw/boards/

Hate to say goodbye to your favorite characters? The perfect solution is a **Synchronized Series!** One world. Three authors. Character cross-over. Triple the amount of books. Binge reading at its best.

Each author's books are full stories you can enjoy individually! But putting them all together weaves an even more pleasurable reading experience.

NINE RULES OF ENGAGEMENT

Roger Patrick isn't in the DEA any longer, but that doesn't mean he's giving up the fight. He's only changing the rules, and in some cases, the target. It didn't matter who that was, even if it was a Henderson.

Gia Gravel has worked hard to get where she is. But when one client crosses the line, she is instantly at risk to lose everything. She's resourceful, and landing a job with the Henderson's, will solve all her problems.

The Hendersons need answers, and will go to any lengths to find them. Roger is the key. When he crosses paths with Gia, he finds himself torn. Where does her loyalty lie?

Gia thought she knew what she wanted. But when Roger enters her life, she questions her choices. Do they need to face their pasts in order to have a future? Or will they break all the rules and follow their hearts?

DEDICATION

This book is dedicated to my sister-in-law and friend Deborah Plante. You have inspired me and so many others. Your smile and positive attitude are contagious. Don't ever lose them!

Karen Lawson and Janet Hitchcock, my editors, you are amazing!

To my readers who continue to inspire me with endless messages and kind words. Always make time for romance.

CHAPTER 1

Gia Gravel couldn't believe it. *Fired?* The word didn't seem possible. Standing on her principles shouldn't mean losing her job.

"You can't be serious. I've been busting my butt for this company, and because I won't tolerate some"—she bit her tongue, thinking piece of shit would be a more accurate description—"some man making a *very* inappropriate proposition."

"Gia, I'm not saying I condone what he said, but your actions were . . . over the top."

"I don't see how a slap across his face was too much." *I actually wanted to kick him in the balls.* At first she thought the jerk had been joking when he'd suggested she get down on her knees. That quickly changed when he grabbed her wrist and pulled her hand to the zipper on his pants. *Disgusting pig.*

"He's one of our biggest clients."

"And that gives him what, the right to abuse your staff?" Gia could feel her heartbeat pounding in her head. This was something you saw on television, but not what you'd expect in your own life.

"I spoke to him. He understands that was . . . inappropriate."

"It was outright wrong. But not as wrong as you still doing business with him." Gia got up from her seat, her blood still boiling, and headed for the door. Turning one last time, she said, "We agree on one thing. I don't want anything to do with you or this place again."

As she stormed out of his office, she knew that wasn't how it would be explained to her colleagues, and unfortunately it was her reputation that would be tarnished. But at least she was leaving with one thing. Her pride.

The moment her feet hit the pavement, the reality of what had just transpired hit her. Gia couldn't remember the last time she was unemployed. She'd been working since she was fifteen, right through college, and, since she graduated, Gia had worked for that company. *And what does my loyalty get me?*

Thankfully the rain had slowed to a drizzle; the showers were supposed to be over by the time she was to leave work, so she hadn't brought an umbrella. The bus came by often enough that she shouldn't get too wet.

But like the rest of her day, it wasn't meant to be. As she rushed toward the bus stop, a dark car flew by. It was too late. She had no time to move. The tires made contact with a puddle, and the water headed in her direction. Within seconds, the cold dirty water covered her from head to toe.

Really? She wanted to scream and stomp her feet. The vehicle stopped, and she saw the reverse lights blink on. They were backing up, but right now, talking to her wasn't really a smart thing to do. Her fuse was short, and she didn't want to take it out on the wrong person. The car stopped beside her and the passenger window rolled down.

A deep voice boomed, "I'm sorry. I didn't see you walking there until it was too late."

That's okay. It's not like I have to return to work. "Thank you. It's only water."

"Let me pay for the dry cleaning," he said, holding out a fifty dollar bill.

She rolled her eyes knowing that was way too much. Her local dry cleaner would only charge five bucks, and her dress was wash-and-wear. Gia didn't bend down to see who she was talking to. It didn't matter. She didn't know him. His car was enough to confirm that. Even her *former* boss didn't drive a Maserati.

"That isn't necessary," Gia said as she continued walking to the bus stop.

The car kept pace with her. "Then at least let me give you a lift to wherever you're heading."

She wasn't born yesterday. There was no way she was getting into a car with a stranger. Money didn't make him a good person; it only made him rich. Without stopping, she replied, "No thank you. I'm all set." She picked up the pace. "Have a good day."

Thankfully the bus had pulled around his car, and she was able to sprint to it. The doors opened and she stepped in. Dropping her token into the box, Gia made her way to the back. Slumping into the seat, she felt her wet dress clinging to her. Looking down she noticed her choice of white today definitely didn't work in her favor. It also explained the looks she had received from the other passengers as she walked down the aisle. Crossing her arms in front of her she glared at the spectators. *Sorry, no free show here.*

It would take about half an hour before the bus

approached her stop. Hopefully her dress would dry some by then. If not, at least she didn't have a long walk, and she knew her neighbors would still all be at work.

Work. This was the worst time to look for a job. All the college kids were out and filling in as interns during the summer. Not that there was a good time to look for work, but some times were better than others. She also didn't have an updated résumé. Until now, she had no idea she'd need one.

She racked her brain thinking of places that might be looking for someone right away. Nothing came to mind. If she waited too long, what happened might get out. Even though she was right, it would work against her. That really pissed her off. A victim shouldn't feel victimized twice. Who would listen to her side of the story? If her boss wouldn't, why would a prospective new employer want to?

Maybe it's time to get the heck out of Boston and go back home. There was something to be said about living in a small town. They didn't really follow what was happening in Boston. They sat around and talked about each other instead. Not in a malicious way, just a nose-in-each-other's-business way. If she moved back to Maplesville, she could tell them she lost her job. The details never needed to come out.

There was no way she'd make enough money in Maplesville to pay for her apartment in Boston. The lease didn't end for another four months. That wasn't a long time, but without a solid income, she would quickly fall behind. There really wasn't a choice. Tomorrow she'd need to seriously find another job here in Boston, even if it was temp work.

Out of the corner of her eye, she saw a few help-wanted signs, but a coffee shop or diner wasn't going to pull in enough to keep her afloat. Trying to smooth out her still wet dress, she laughed to herself. *Maybe I should've taken that*

4

fifty. Actually if enough people splashed and paid her, she might just make enough to make it a business.

The bus pulled over, but it didn't appear to be one of the usual spots. She watched as the driver got out and went around to the back of the bus. She swore she heard some cussing going on in the back, and by the look on the driver's face what he returned, she understood why.

"Sorry, ladies and gentlemen, but the bus has a flat tire. I called, and it will be almost two hours before another bus is available to come and transport. But they will be towing the bus shortly, so I'll need to ask you all to exit the bus."

That was ridiculous. They were in the business section of town. There were taxis everywhere, but actually getting one to stop wasn't easy, and it was going to be expensive if she wanted it to take her all the way home. She always watched her spending, and now would need to more than ever.

Totally frustrated, Gia grabbed her purse and did as she was asked. Her shoulders, normally held high, now slumped. Was this day ever going to end? Or if she was lucky, maybe it hadn't started and all this was only a horrible dream.

The moment she stepped onto the sidewalk the sky opened and rain came down in buckets instead of droplets. She looked around for shelter. There were a few small trees planted curbside, but they were more for show than anything. If there had been a coffee shop or café, Gia would've scooted in and bought a coffee, which would also buy her time until the other bus arrived.

But there were only tall buildings, all offices, with *no loitering* signs posted all around. Her dream was to work in one of those someday. Standing in front, looking like a wet cat, wasn't the first impression she'd want to make. So she did the only thing she could. She started walking toward the closest bus stop to hop on another bus.

As she passed one of the tallest buildings, she noticed a familiar vehicle illegally parked in front. It could be a coincidence or a different car all together. She hoped he wasn't following her because that would be too creepy. As she made her way by, she crouched down and looked inside. It was empty. *I should've known. Too rich to care about following the rules.*

Gia wished she could take that no parking sign down and put it on his windshield. *Maybe through it.*

She realized once again her frustration from the scumbag at work was being taken out on this stranger. People illegally parked, double parked, and heck sometimes totally blocked the road. None of it was her concern. She was angry at the universe for not playing fair. Maybe when she got home, took off her wet clothes, and had a hot cup of tea, things might look better.

As another car, this time a limo, came by and once again splashed her, she thought, *maybe a glass of wine instead.*

"You really need to talk to Bennett," Brice Henderson said.

There was no way in hell he was working for Bennett or any of the Hendersons. He never wanted to feel indebted to anyone, especially a family like theirs. The Hendersons may have come out clean this time, but they were far from without blemish. As far as Roger Patrick was concerned, there wasn't anything to discuss. It was over, and it seemed as though the Hendersons were one big happy family. He shook his head and replied, "I'm not the work-for-someone-else type of guy."

"We could use someone with your . . . talents on our team."

Roger heard the difference. How it changed from Bennett

to "we." That's how the Hendersons worked. They took care of each other above anyone else.

"From what I heard, you have plenty of people in your . . . pocket already." He wasn't sure if the Hendersons had any idea how much he knew about them. He'd done a lot of digging for his best friend, Caydan Pintino. Which of course abruptly ceased once Caydan found out he was a Henderson by blood. Roger still found all this fucked up and disturbing.

"I'd like to tell you you're wrong. We're not known for always . . . playing nice. Then again, you're not either. We haven't forgotten your part in trying to bring down the New Hope Resort," Brice said.

Roger wasn't going to deny it. Hell, he'd crossed the line several times helping Caydan. He was good at his job and actually a bit shocked the Hendersons knew it had been him. *Most likely they're just guessing.* "Your point?" he asked, glaring at Brice. Their money and power didn't impress or intimidate him. If anything, he knew it made them a better target. That's all.

"I'd like to think we could be on the same side now."

"I'm not for or against your family," Roger responded. That was the truth. They weren't his enemy. But for a long time, they were Caydan's. He was happy his friend had found his family. That didn't mean Roger trusted them, and his loyalty still was with Caydan. *If things go wrong, Caydan isn't the only person you'll answer to.*

"That's good to hear, because I'd like to hire you."

"I already told you, I'm not the team type," Roger snarled.

"I know. And that's what I'm looking for. This is personal, and I need someone I can trust."

Roger laughed. "And you believe you can trust me? Why?"

"You're not the only one who has done his research."

There were things in Roger's past he didn't want to discuss. Things he wished he'd done differently. They haunted him to this day. But going back and second chances weren't possible. At least not for him. Some things were unfixable.

"Brice, save us both time. Tell me what the hell you want. If I'm interested, I'll let you know."

Brice stared at Roger for a moment as though he wasn't sure what to say. That piqued Roger's interest. "I want a full genealogy done on my family."

"You don't need me for that," Roger stated. "Hire a genealogist."

"Can't do that."

"Why?" Roger asked.

"When you dig, sometimes you find shit you don't want anyone to know."

Roger had discovered enough of that when he did the research on them. Skeletons in a closet had an entirely different meaning with them. He wasn't sure he wanted to know any more.

"If you're looking for trouble, I'm sure it will eventually find you." One thing he'd learned: the Hendersons didn't stay out of the public eye for long. Rarely was it anything good either. Something or someone always stirred the pot, and he didn't want his name associated with them when shit hit the fan.

"And that's why I need you. Finding out that we . . . that I have an older brother was a shock."

Never mind knowing how that all came about. James Henderson was one sick mother fucker. He hated the man even though he'd never met him. But what he'd done to Caydan's mother was unforgivable. Roger cared for her as though she were his own mother, and she accepted him as family as well. But there was a part of him that struggled to deal with everything he'd learned. *And I'm not really family.*

"Are you worried Caydan is going to take your spot as head of the family? Because I've known him quite a while, and trust me, he doesn't want it." Roger was shocked at how welcoming they had all been to Caydan. *Too welcoming.*

"If he did, he could have it. It comes with burdens I wish I didn't bear," Brice said, shaking his head. "It's not what we know that concerns me. Every time I think I've heard the worst of it, I find out I'm wrong. My family can't keep going through this. We can't change the past, but we can't keep getting blindsided either. It's no longer just the six of us. We're married with children. None of us want this shit to fall on them. Not if we can help it."

He'd met the entire family at Caydan and Allyson's wedding a few months ago. Roger knew he wouldn't do this for Brice or his other siblings. But, for Caydan and his nephews and nieces, he'd at least hear Brice out on exactly what he needed.

"Does this mean you need me to head back to Tabiq?" Roger asked.

"That's the problem. I'm not sure where to start looking." Brice pulled out a black and white photo of two children. It was in poor condition. The time period wasn't James's generation.

"Who is this?"

"That's why I need you."

This really wasn't much to go on. "Where did you find it?" Brice had to know something if he was willing to go to this length.

"I was the one who cleaned out our father's personal belongings. This was in a box I hadn't seen before."

"What else was in there?" Roger wanted to see the box and exam it himself.

"Papers from my father's early school years. Progress report cards and a few things I assume he made for his mother, my grandmother. I'm not sure. He spoke very little about her. My father said she was all we had as family. But we both know James Henderson was capable of more evil than anyone imagined. I'm sure lying was a way of life for him."

Roger had come across some real fucking assholes in his DEA years. None had come close to what he'd learned about James. That was his concern with Brice and the others. Unlike Caydan, they'd grown up under the same roof as that asshole. He knew what Caydan was capable of, the type of person he was. The rest of the family, he wasn't so sure about.

"To do what you're asking means digging deeper into your family's history. Are you okay with me seeing things you don't want the world to know?" It was going to be impossible to determine who was in that photo without coming across a lot of confidential information regarding the Henderson clan. *If it even was a Henderson.*

"As long as you keep me updated on everything you find, then yes."

The hairs still stood up on the back of his neck. Why did Brice want him? It made no sense that he wasn't utilizing the connections he already had. People they had a history with. *Ones they so-called trusted.*

"I thought you had the Turchettas doing your dirty work," Roger said. "I'm sure this shit is right up Gabe's alley."

"Normally, yes. We worked very closely on addressing certain issues back in Tabiq. But they also have some . . . family things they need to attend to. Besides, they have become quite close with the family. For the moment, I'd like to keep this quiet."

Roger understood why Brice might not want strangers to know, but he needed clarification. "So you don't want *anyone*, not even your brothers to know?"

"Not even Caydan," Brice said firmly.

And this is why I don't trust you. Lying to Caydan wasn't something Roger had ever done. That's not how friends remained friends. But Caydan found a brother and family. If taking on this job meant Roger would protect his friend, he would swallow his pride and do it.

"Do you think you can do this?" Brice asked.

"You know I can, otherwise you wouldn't have brought me to Boston. Are you only looking for who is in the picture or *everything* I can uncover about your family's legacy?"

With a heavy sigh, Brice reluctantly said, "Everything."

Roger stood. "I hope you won't regret what you're doing."

"My life has been filled with regret. That's why I'm doing this now. I've had this picture for a few years. It's time to find out why my father had it."

Slipping the photo into the breast pocket of his suit, Roger said, "You can't pay me enough to figure out what your father had been thinking. But I'll get you the answer on who's in the picture. Not promising anything more than that."

When he left Brice's office, he ran into Bennett Stone, who seemed surprised to see him there.

"Are you lost?" Bennett asked.

Roger shook his head. He understood why Bennett didn't like or trust him. He, after all, had managed to do what no one else had. *Fucked with the Henderson family without getting caught.* If it hadn't been for Caydan wanting to come clean with everything, wanting to show a good faith effort with his siblings, they still wouldn't know shit.

"I didn't know you were back in Boston," Roger said, avoiding the question.

"It's my home. Unlike you, that is."

"That might change."

Bennett cocked a brow. "You're moving to Boston. Why?"

Roger smirked. "Easier for me to keep an eye on you."

Bennett didn't seem amused. "Vice versa."

He laughed. "Trust me, my life isn't half as interesting as the family you married into."

"There's more to them than you realize."

And seems like more than you do as well. "At least that's one thing we agree on. Now if you don't mind, I have some things to take care of."

Bennett stayed, blocking his way. "I hope whatever it is, it doesn't involve fucking with my family."

"If I was, trust me, I wouldn't be here right now." With that, Roger pushed past Bennett and headed for the elevator. It was going to be a lot easier to keep things under wrap if he wasn't so damn visible.

If he'd known what Brice wanted to discuss, he would've suggested they *not* meet at Henderson Towers. Although the family each had their own businesses, they frequented that place all too often. If he didn't get out of there, the odds of meeting up with another one increased.

Sure enough, just before he left the building he bumped into Lena, Brice's wife. "Aren't you Caydan's friend? Roger, I believe."

Smiling, he said, "You have a very good memory."

"I used to have a better one. Now with two children, I seem to only remember what they need to go to next. Our oldest, Nicholas, is almost eight, and I'm not sure whose schedule is busier, his or Brice's."

"I have a feeling the correct answer is . . . yours."

Lena laughed. "You are so right." She rested a hand on her well rounded stomach and said, "I don't know what I'm going to do when this little one comes along. That's why I'm here. We have an ultrasound appointment."

"Here?" Roger asked.

Lena shook her head. "No. But Brice was tied up in a meeting, and I couldn't wait any longer. Really, I hate to cut this short, but I have to go."

She waved a hand, and he watched as she waddled her way to the restroom. Roger knew he was the reason Brice was late to meet Lena.

Although Brice said no one, that wasn't going to happen. So far two people knew he was there. Roger was going to need to act quickly if he was going to get any answers for Brice before the entire family started asking questions.

That meant Roger was going to make sure the people he utilized weren't ones the Hendersons had or might have crossed paths with. *Damn it. I'm going to have to call in some favors to pull this off. I hate wasting them on a Henderson.*

He left the building, grabbed the parking ticket, and climbed into his Maserati. He still felt bad about leaving that woman in a dress that shouldn't be worn when wet. *And she sure as hell shouldn't have worn a pink bra underneath.* But that wasn't his problem. He'd done all he could do to make amends, and she didn't want any help. *If she had taken my offer for a ride, the meeting with Brice would've run a lot later.*

Roger wished he could turn his back from someone in need. His life sure as hell would be a lot quieter if he could. His gut told him that woman was upset about more than his

13

splashing her. If he hadn't been rushing to meet Brice, he'd have pulled over, gotten out of the car, and spoken to her face to face. The end result might have been the same. *Guess I'll never know.* It was too late. She was probably long gone, and the odds of seeing her again were slim to none. Besides, he'd given his word to help Brice. There was only a short window of time to pull off what Brice was asking. It was a waste of time to think about a woman when he didn't even know her name.

Let's keep this as uncomplicated as possible, so I can get the heck out of Boston.

CHAPTER 2

Gia had to admit, getting splashed by a limo yesterday was really the only good thing that happened to her. The poor woman who had gotten out looked like she should be on her way to the hospital to deliver instead of rushing into an office building. But she had taken the time to insist the driver give Gia a lift home.

Now as she sat on her couch, she couldn't believe she hadn't given a second thought to getting into the limo. That was crazy. Was it because she had felt beaten down by that time? Surely it wasn't because she had felt any safer. They were all strangers to her. Yet it was strangers who were being thoughtful. *Someone I thought I knew . . . only thought of his wallet.*

Gia refused to let that situation pull her down again today. Being positive was her nature, and all the negative energy from yesterday needed to be left where it was. *In the past.* She had spent her morning updating her résumé then uploading it to different sites. She felt confident she'd get a call, if not right away, then later in the week.

She had done all she could for one day. The only thing

left was to clean her apartment. It definitely needed some TLC. Gia had been working so much she couldn't recall the last time she'd dusted. As she ran her finger over the coffee table, she cringed. *Way too long.*

Housework would keep her mind occupied. Then again, so would reading a good book. She was just about to close her laptop and get to work when an email notification came in. As soon as she opened the email she knew it was too good to be true. It was a scam. For five hundred dollars they could ensure she was placed in a job within twenty-four hours. She hit delete and closed the laptop.

Now dusting was even less appealing. Gia got up and looked for her purse. She took her reading tablet to work every day, thinking she'd read during her lunch break. That never happened. Now there wasn't anything stopping her.

Where the hell did I put it? She tried retracing her steps. She had been so upset when she got home she stripped down in the bathroom and tossed her clothes in the hamper. Had she grabbed her purse and thrown it in too?

Gia dumped out everything and found nothing but dirty laundry. Wherever she put her purse, it wasn't out in the open. *I made tea.* Walking over, she looked in the cupboards. Nothing out of the ordinary there. *A bowl of cereal.* She opened the refrigerator and still nothing.

She had to have left it in the limo yesterday afternoon. But if they'd found it, surely they would've reached out and let her know. At least if it was her, she'd open it to find out who it belonged to.

Great. Now I have to find a limo company without a clue where to start.

That wasn't totally true. Someone in that building might know the woman who had been dropped off. If she could find her, she might find her purse. That was progress.

Gia quickly changed from her bum-around-the-house clothes to a pair of white slacks and a light blue silk blouse. She wasn't walking through the business district or entering that building without looking as though she belonged there. *Who knows, maybe I'll meet my next boss there.*

She tried to think positive, that everything happened for a reason. Since the day before had been nothing but crap, she hoped this one would make up for it. Gia snickered. *I'll be happy if I can just locate my purse and everything is intact.* If she were to be offered a job somewhere, she was going to need her identification.

Gia hoped her phone wouldn't ring, at least not right then. It wasn't as though her job had been critical, but it did require her to pay close attention to detail. *Who would hire me if I can't keep track of my crap, never mind theirs?* She didn't make mistakes as a compliance auditor. Normally she was the one looking for someone else's.

As she looked at herself in the mirror, she couldn't help but feel angry at herself. Gia had the habit of focusing so intensely on her work she missed things happening around her by shutting out the office noise. That was how the client had been able to catch her off guard. She should be more aware of her surroundings.

If I had been, maybe I'd have noticed my purse sitting on the seat.

Since she didn't have her wallet, she had to pull cash out of her emergency fund before grabbing her keys and cell phone.

At least she had money to get around for a few days. If things got out of control and went on longer, she might have to reach out to her parents and ask to borrow some until she could get another bank card.

Looking at her watch, she realized she better get her butt

17

moving before the office closed. She hopped on the bus and within twenty minutes she was across from Henderson Towers. She looked around in case the limo was parked nearby. She giggled as there were several on the street. There was nothing to distinguish one from the other. So she was forced to go inside.

Immediately she was greeted by a security guard. "May I help you?"

"Yes, I'm . . . ah . . . I'm looking for a woman who was here yesterday about this same time."

"Do you have her name?" he asked.

"No I don't. But she has long blonde hair and was very pregnant."

The man looked at her. "And you are?"

"Gia Gravel."

"Do you have an appointment?" She shook her head. "Can I see some identification?"

She didn't realize it would be so difficult to find out if anyone had her purse. "I don't have any with me."

"Then I can't help you," he said firmly.

"But you don't understand. I need to ask her something."

He crossed his arms and looked at her. She couldn't see behind his dark glasses, but she bet his eyes matched his "ain't gonna fucking happen lady" body language. She'd been bullied yesterday by two men. No way was he making it three.

"I'm not asking to go inside. All I want is to know who she is. She gave me a ride home yesterday, and I believe I left something in her limo."

"I'm sure if you did, she'll return it to you."

He was unwavering, but so was she. "Then can you tell me if she works here?"

A deep voice from behind her said, "Depends on why you want to know."

And here we go again. She spun around, ready to start the conversation from the beginning if she had to, but the security guard said, "I suggest you tell her nothing."

The guy didn't seem interested one bit in what he was being told. "What's your name?"

"Gia. Yesterday it was raining, and I was wet, and this really nice woman offered me a ride home. But I think I left my purse in her limo."

He cocked a brow as he asked, "You got in her vehicle? Why?"

"I was wet and cold, and she was kind enough to offer me a ride." *Not that I need to explain my actions to you.*

"Are you positive she has your purse? Because I'd like to believe she'd reach out to you if she did."

"That's what I told her," the security guard interjected.

Gia shot him a look. He didn't want to help, so he should butt out and let the guy, who seemed interested, help.

"Well, I'm not one hundred percent positive, but I know I don't have it, and her limo was the last place I was."

"Then let's go find out."

"Hey. I can't let you do that," the guard said.

The man looked at him and said, "I don't believe I asked you. If you have any questions, call Mr. Henderson. But right now, Gia is with me."

It almost sounded like the guard growled. Instead of going farther into the building, he waved for her to follow him back outside. "Where are we going?"

"To find out if she has your purse."

Gia stopped and asked, "You do know who she is, right?"

"Yes. Lena Henderson, married to Brice Henderson.

Funny that I know more about her and yet you were the one who got in her car."

"I don't see how that is odd. She offered me a ride and I got in."

"Why did she do that?" he asked.

Being honest wasn't going to hurt. "I was walking, and her vehicle splashed me."

"I'm having a difficult time believing you."

Her eyes widened. "Excuse me. Why would I lie about such a thing?"

"First of all, I know for a fact that Lena didn't leave with you. She left with Brice."

He was right. "I didn't mean she gave me the ride home personally. But she asked her driver to give me a ride."

"So you got into the limo with a guy you didn't know?"

"Yes. I know. It's foolish, but as I said, I was cold and wet."

"Well, what is your excuse now? You're out here with me in search of your purse and you don't know me, not even my name."

Gia crossed her arms. *Arrogant ass.* "Who said I was going anywhere with you?"

"I thought you wanted to find out about your purse?"

She did. But then again, she also wanted to stay alive. "Not that badly."

"You're a very . . . interesting woman, Gia."

Somehow she didn't think he meant that as a compliment. "Are you going to introduce yourself or just continue being rude?"

"Roger."

First name was better than nothing. "And you know Lena how?" She didn't know why she was asking. Was she making small talk until she could come up with a reason to walk away? That was almost as ridiculous as this so called conversation. Roger didn't really seem to want to help her as much as he wanted to question her.

"I'm a friend of the family."

"Oh. Then maybe you can call her for me and ask."

"That's my plan." He pulled out his cell phone and made a call.

This might be easier than I thought. Well, now at least. But that was short-lived. When the call ended he said, "Sorry, they haven't seen it. Are you sure it was there?"

"That or on the bus."

"Did you try calling them?" Roger asked.

She shook her head. "No, I can do that now." But the bus she'd been on had been towed. That meant they might not have located her purse yet. Or worse, it was lost for good. She traveled with all her identification inside her purse. Gia panicked as she searched for the bus terminal's number. After being put on hold for what seemed like an eternity, she finally got through to an actual person instead of a computer.

"Hello. My name is Gia Gravel. I was on bus one zero-nine yesterday, and I just realized I may have left my purse inside."

"Miss, that bus is in the repair shop."

"I'm aware of that." *Since I was on it when the tire blew.* "But I need someone to check for my purse."

"We don't have anyone who can do that. The bus should be returned to us sometime tomorrow. If you would like, I can have someone check for you then."

She tried not to let her frustration show as she could feel Roger watching her while she spoke. *Be professional. Be respectful. Hell, be assertive!* "I can't wait that long. This is my purse we're talking about, not a book."

"Miss, I understand that, but the repair shop will be

closing soon. The best I can do is look for you tomorrow. I'm sorry."

Roger waved for her phone, and she looked at him like he was crazy. "I promise, I'll give it back." Reluctantly she handed him her phone. "Who am I talking to?"

Roger's tone was much more . . . demanding and firm than hers had been. She wished she could hear the response.

"I believe Miss Gravel has asked nicely. If I need to go there and look myself, you won't get the same from me." Gia could hear some grumbling on the other end of the line before Roger continued. "I'll wait."

As they waited, she was shocked and perturbed. Why did it take a man to get the guy's butt moving? No one should have to threaten to get action. *So much for, you can catch more flies with honey. Maybe you get more with a swatter.*

Although they didn't have an answer yet, she still appreciated Roger for trying. "Thank you."

"Haven't done anything yet," Roger replied.

"You got him to at least look. That's something."

"The guy's an ass."

And you're a . . . She wasn't sure what word would best describe him. If he got them to locate her purse, she might need to change her initial thought to hero.

Roger raised a finger as he was back on the phone. "Good. Tell them we will be there in about thirty minutes."

"They have it?" she asked. He nodded.

"I don't give a shit what time they close. If they value their job, they will have someone there waiting for us." Roger handed the phone back to her. "You ready?"

"For what?"

"To go to the repair shop. They've located your purse," Roger said.

"And you really think there will be someone there after

hours?" If she had made the request, the answer would've been no.

"There will be."

"Thank you. I better head over to the—"

"We."

"What?"

Roger said, "We will head over. It is a half hour drive." He looked down at her. "I assume you're not driving since you didn't have your purse."

"I was going to take the bus."

He shook his head. "My car isn't far."

"I don't take rides from strangers," she said firmly.

"We both know that isn't true. You took one yesterday from Lena."

"That was different," she replied, defending her actions.

"If it would make you feel better, I can splash you again with my car."

"Again?" she asked. Roger pointed to a black car parked not far from them. "That was you?"

He nodded. "Unfortunately, yesterday didn't seem to be your day. I'm hoping you will allow me to make it up to you by giving you a ride to retrieve your belongings."

"That really isn't necessary."

"I disagree. The shop is closing, and I'm your best option to get there."

My only option to get there. She didn't have enough cash to pay a cab for that distance.

"I guess it will be okay."

She let him lead the way to his car. She almost hated to sit on the fine leather seat. At least she wasn't soaking wet today.

As they pulled away, Roger said, "You should've let me give you a ride yesterday."

"I was . . . a bit . . . distracted at that time."

"Pissed might be a better term."

She snickered. "And that still wouldn't be strong enough. But it didn't have anything to do with getting splashed."

"Want to talk about it?" Roger asked.

No. But then again, she needed to talk about something. Sitting in the car, staring out the window, was kind of awkward. It wasn't like she was ever going to see him again so what did it matter?

"I just got fired."

He gave her a quick look and then his eyes were back on the busy road. "That would do it. What is it that you do . . . did?"

"Compliance auditor."

"I have no idea what that means."

"I go through documents and procedures to ensure a company is complying with the government or company guidelines. Really not all that exciting to most people, but I love the research aspect."

"What did you do, miss something?"

"Excuse me?"

"You said you got fired. I assume you missed something," Roger stated.

"And you'd be assuming incorrectly. *I* didn't do anything wrong," she snapped.

"I think I just did. I'm sorry."

"It's a sore subject for me. My boss . . . he didn't support me the way I expected he would."

"What happened?" Roger asked.

She didn't want to get into being sexually harassed in the workplace. There were other ways to get her point across. "He values money more than he does work ethics." *Or his employees.*

"There are a lot of people driven by greed."

She looked at his Maserati. He surely wasn't hurting for cash. "Yes, there are." Gia heard her sarcastic tone and wished she could take it back.

"I deserve that."

"I don't know you so I can't, or shouldn't at least, presume to know."

Roger laughed. "I'm a lot of things, Gia, but greedy isn't one of them." He brought the subject back to her. "What are you going to do for work now?"

"I'm sure I'll find something." The only question she had was how long finding the right job would take. She didn't want to make a rash decision and be stuck working for a jerk.

Thankfully they pulled up in front of the repair shop. The sign clearly said closed. But Roger didn't seem fazed by it at all. He got out of the car and asked, "Are you coming?"

"I think we're too late."

"They are there," he said confidently.

She what she'd seen so far, he was used to getting what he wanted. *Must be nice.* Gia opened the door and went with him to the entrance. Roger didn't even knock. A greasy mechanic greeted him, holding her purse.

"This must belong to you," he said, handing the purse to Roger.

She couldn't help but chuckle. Rogers's expression was priceless. Gia could tell he was holding back some explicit words.

"Everything better be inside," Roger warned as he took the purse and handed it to her.

"I didn't even open it," he replied.

Roger turned to Gia and asked, "Do you want to look through it while we're here?"

Gia looked at the mechanic who seemed nervous. She

didn't think it had anything to do with things missing as much as it did with Roger's demeanor. The look in his eyes made the security guard from before look like a pussy cat.

She opened it and looked quickly. "Seems in order."

"Good." Roger turned to the mechanic and handed him some money. Gia tried to see how much, but it was too late. The cash had been quickly pocketed.

As they headed back to Roger's car, she said, "You didn't need to do that, you know. I have my purse back and could've tipped him."

"Since you wouldn't let me pay for your dry cleaning, this is the least I can do."

She smiled. "It was wash-and-wear."

"I'm glad it wasn't ruined. You looked—"

"Wet." She didn't want any bullshit line about looking nice.

"You say it as it is. That's refreshing."

"Wish my boss had thought so," Gia muttered.

"His loss."

Gia laughed. "Yes, it is. Except I will miss having a pay check." She might not live a wild lifestyle, but food in the fridge, a roof over her head, and clothes on her back were nice.

"I have a feeling you won't be unemployed for long," Roger stated.

As she got back inside his car she said softly, "I hope not."

They were almost back to Henderson Tower when Roger asked, "Would you like to have dinner with me?"

Her stomach was growling, and he probably was only showing pity on her. Just as he'd seemed to since they'd crossed paths again. "You don't need to do that."

"Eat? My stomach says otherwise."

She shook her head. "Ask me to dinner. You can drop me off anywhere, and I can find my way home."

Roger laughed. "First off, I don't do anything I don't want to. Second, it's just dinner. Either you're hungry or you're not, but I'd enjoy the company."

She wasn't sure what they would talk about, but she knew there was nothing to eat at home. Normally she ate toast and tea for breakfast and ate out for lunch. That had come and gone, and one thing Roger was right about, she needed to eat.

"Only if I can pick the place."

He cocked a brow then said, "Just give me the directions."

Roger had no idea what he was doing sitting in a pizza joint when he had shit he was supposed to be working on. But he'd been so shocked to see Gia standing in Henderson Towers arguing with the security guard. No matter how tough she was, there was no way she would've gotten through. The Hendersons would've fired the guard's ass if she had. Of course, Roger wasn't technically on the payroll. More like doing them a favor. Not that he had any plans of collecting on it later. But he opened his mouth then wished he could take it back.

"Give me your résumé and I'll pass it along to the Hendersons." Her eyes widened with hope and he couldn't back out now. "Not sure if they are looking for anyone with your skill set."

"You'd really do that for me?" Gia asked.

He nodded. "I can only get it in their hands. After that, it will up to you to sell yourself to them, if they want you." Gia laughed and Roger didn't know what was so funny. "Questioning your abilities?"

Shaking her head, she answered, "I think I've changed my mind about rainy days. They're not as bad as I had thought."

He could appreciate her positive attitude. Roger would be shocked if the Hendersons didn't take her on. But even as he thought about it, he wondered what the hell was wrong with him. Gia seemed so nice, sweet and honest. Those guys weren't going to appreciate what she had to offer. It actually was possible she'd have the same, if not worse, experience than with her last boss.

"I'm looking for help on a project."

"I'll find a job. I don't need you making one up because you feel bad for me."

This time Roger laughed. "You seem to think I'm a lot nicer person than I really am."

"Maybe it's because you've gone out of your way for me today. Jerks usually don't do things like this."

"Maybe I'm a wolf in sheep's clothing."

Gia took a sip of her grape soda and then asked, "Is this your way of saying you *don't* want me to work for you? That's the worse sales pitch I've ever heard."

Roger answered, "Unfortunately, it's the truth."

"Not that I'm not grateful for the . . . offer, but I really need something steady. And there's no way I could commit to a project. If the right job came along, I'd feel obligated to finish it instead of doing what was best for me."

A good work ethic was yet another reason he knew the Hendersons would hire her. If it was Caydan, that wouldn't be an issue. But Caydan was still in Tabiq. Roger wasn't going to ask if she'd be interested in relocating. His fear was she'd say yes. Things were improving, but it still wasn't a place he'd send anyone. Especially not someone like Gia. He had a tough exterior, but he was good at reading people. She was fragile inside. Something, or someone, had hurt her.

"I tell you what. Here is my number. If you change your mind, give me a call. I won't hold you to any restrictions, except one."

"And what is that?" Gia asked as she took the business card.

"You always do what is best for you."

She looked at him then smiled. "Deal. But you know I still have no idea what it is you do."

"I help people." That was the very short version. How, what, and why didn't need to be disclosed. At least not to her.

"That's vague."

"I work on some very confidential things. The project I'm suggesting would be one of them. You would only be given limited information and asked to research strictly from that."

"I won't do anything illegal," Gia stated firmly.

Roger nodded. "Good. Because I won't be asking you to. Think about it. If you're interested, call."

Gia slipped the card in her purse and said, "I really don't think I'll be unemployed that long."

"I agree."

"And you're really okay if I can't give you a two-week notice?"

"I am," Roger said. He didn't want a long-term employee, and this seemed perfect. Gia had already connected with Lena, and he might be able to use that to his benefit. He needed a way into the family besides using Caydan. "Are you married or have a boyfriend?"

Gia arched her brow. "You know that's illegal to ask a potential employee."

"I said *you* wouldn't be doing anything illegal, never said I don't work in a . . . gray area."

"No husband, No boyfriend. How about yourself?"

"Neither. And actually, I'm not looking for either."

"Then why the question?" Gia asked.

"Because I don't want *anyone* to know you're assisting me. If we are seen together, and I'm forced to introduce you, I might—"

"Say I'm your wife?" Gia asked, her tone high-pitched.

"I was going to say date, maybe girlfriend depending on the situation. Wife is a bit . . . permanent."

"Oh, you're one of those."

He cocked a brow. "Liar?"

"No, noncommittal."

Roger laughed. "Actually I'm a person who knows what he wants. I'm not opposed to marriage. It's just not for me."

"I can see how your private, confidential life might get in the way. Wives don't like secrets."

There's a lot of things a wife wouldn't like about me. Roger didn't consider himself a total asshole, but close enough. A relationship took compromise, and that wasn't something he did very well. Yet he was doing just that with Gia. Was it really compromise or was he just helping someone in need? There were other ways to accomplish that. Hell, he could've given her money to hold her over until she found a job. None of this was his issue nor his concern. So why not just drop her ass off and drive away?

Maybe it was because she didn't swoon over his car. Hell, he'd bet if it'd been any other woman he'd splashed and offered money or a ride, they'd have taken him up on one if not both of them. But Gia hadn't. She wanted to make it on her own by her terms, even though she might be getting in her own way. He respected that. And offering her this so called job was his way of doing it with her feeling in control.

"Then I guess we are in agreement that single is the right status for me."

"I'd need to know you better to make that assumption,"

Gia said then quickly added, "But then again, I'd like to keep this strictly professional, if you don't mind."

"Does that mean you're taking this job?"

Gia nodded. "I guess so. When would you like to start?"

Today was a loss as far as getting her onboard. "How does tomorrow morning sound?"

"I'll be ready. Where do you want me to meet you?"

"Why don't I pick you up?" Roger asked.

Gia finished her pizza before asking, "Do you pick up all your employees?" Roger grinned and shook his head. "Then there's no reason to make *me* the exception." She wrote her number on a piece of paper and handed it to him. "Just text me the time and location, and I'll meet you there."

Damn, you're stubborn. Roger hoped that was something he could use in his favor. Brice said *he* couldn't be in contact with the family, and he wouldn't. *Gia will.*

Roger slipped the number into his pocket and said, "At least let me give you a ride home."

Thankfully she agreed, because he wasn't going to let her hop a bus at this late hour. Then again, he hadn't realized she lived so close to the pizza parlor. Maybe that was why she had picked that place. If shit went bad and she wanted out, she didn't have far to go.

Good. Keep your wits about you and you'll go far. It's ruthless in the business world, and those sharks are waiting to eat you up. He knew too damn well from experience just how far some people were willing to go to get what they wanted. When he worked for the DEA, there were rules to engage with those assholes. But now he worked for himself, and the only rules were the ones he set.

Rule one. Remember, you're only helping her until she finds work. Hands off.

31

CHAPTER 3

Gia thought for sure she'd be up all night long after her panic attack over her purse. Instead she found herself sleeping so soundly she almost missed Roger's text message. Thankfully he wasn't asking her to meet him anytime soon. She had time to shower, dress, and catch a bus.

For someone like Roger, a car might make sense. Odds were the police weren't going to ticket his luxury vehicle. But she wouldn't be able to pay the fines associated with illegal parking. And a parking garage was too costly. By the end of the day, she'd be working strictly to pay for a car. That made no sense to her. Besides, the public transit system got her everyplace she needed to go. Hopefully, whatever she was going to be doing for Roger would be on their routes as well.

She had no clue why Roger was willing to take her on, not knowing how long she was going to be able to work for him. He didn't strike her as someone who'd risk being left in a lurch. Then again, what did he know about her in the first place? Everything she told him could've been a lie. It wasn't, but how would he know that?

Gia wasn't sure who was being more foolish: Roger for

32

hiring her or her for agreeing to his offer. She knew if it seemed too good to be true, it probably was. And then the whole thing about claiming her as a date if they were caught out in public, that was just . . . a strange request.

He was rich and attractive. There was no way anyone was going to believe he was on a date with her. She didn't consider herself ugly, but she pictured him with someone who pampered herself with expensive salons and pricey clothes. If she didn't find it on a clearance rack, you better believe she found it at a consignment shop. Paying full price, never mind a high price, wasn't in her DNA.

Gia grew up in a large family of five older siblings and one younger. Her parents taught her the value of a penny. She didn't toss them aside, they added up, and sometimes that jar of coins was all they had to buy milk and bread. Even though both her parents had worked, it seemed one of the kids always needed something that hadn't been in the budget.

That's why she had to make this happen. Going back home was an option, and her parents said the door was always open, but they had sacrificed enough. It wasn't fair to them to be a burden, not at her age. Knowing she had their support was good enough. It had to be.

Since she had no idea what kind of work she was going to be doing—it could be cleaning his house for all she knew— she was going to dress business casual. Like the day they first met, or made contact through the puddle, she opted for a dress and sandals. The weatherman said it was going to be a clear and sunny day. However, in New England the weather changed in the blink of an eye.

Believing she was dressed for almost anything, Gia headed to the café that Roger asked to meet at. She wasn't a coffee drinker, and this place was known for their espresso. Hopefully they also served hot tea.

When she got off the bus, she knew Roger was already there. That black sleek beast was parked directly in front, but as she walked closer, she noticed he was sitting inside. He was on his cell phone, and the way he slapped his steering wheel, things weren't going the way he wanted. He'd made it clear he wasn't all that . . . nice. Was this a more accurate view of who he really was?

What did she know about him, except he was somehow linked with the Hendersons? That had been made clear when he called Lena and used her first name without any introduction. That was the only reference he'd come with.

It wasn't as though she personally knew any of the Hendersons, but there was no way you lived or worked in Boston and didn't know of them. Several families were that rich and powerful. Hendersons and Barringtons were two of the top ten. *And Roger says he's going to get my résumé in their hands.*

She hadn't forgotten that and had a copy prepared and with her. Hopefully his word was worth as much as his car.

Standing outside while he chewed out whomever he was talking to didn't make any sense. So she went inside and ordered a black leaf tea with honey. She was about to pay when she noticed orange pecan scones drizzled with a sugar glaze. Having one heated and added to her bill, she grabbed them both and took a seat beside the window. It provided her a great view of him sitting in his car.

From the scowl on his face, it didn't look as though he was going to be entering the café any time soon. Even if he blew her off, it wasn't a total loss. The scone was delicious.

A man she didn't know came over and asked, "Is this seat taken?"

Gia looked up and said, "I'm . . . waiting for someone."

"Why don't I keep you company in case they don't show."

Roger's deep voice said, "Take a hint. She's not interested." The guy turned around and was about to utter something else, but for some reason, he clamped his mouth shut and walked away.

Smart man. She wished it had something to do with her, but she knew it was the look in Roger's eyes. There was something menacing, and only a fool would push to find out how far he'd go. She wasn't about to flatter herself and think he was jealous that another man was showing interest. Although his tone was one of a jealous boyfriend, she knew Roger had been pissed off before he entered the building. So she bit back any sarcastic teasing as the timing was off. The last thing she wanted was to add to what already seemed to be a bad day.

Gia let it drop. "I don't know how you take your coffee or I'd have gotten you one."

"I'm good, but normally, strong and black," he said as he took a seat. "I had a few things to take care of."

Yes you did. She hoped she'd never feel his wrath. "It gave me a chance to have a bite to eat."

"I guess we can get started." He reached inside his pocket, pulled out a photo, and handed it to her. "What do you know about photography?"

She looked at the black and white picture. "That it has changed a lot since this was taken." She continued to hold onto it as she asked, "Who are they?"

"I don't know."

"I guess the first thing would be find out when and where it was taken. That might help you find out who they are," Gia stated.

"Anything else to add?" Roger asked.

"What do you have to go on besides the photo?" Gia loved a mystery, but this might be more than she was prepared for. Usually she would be looking through documents and files to find an inconsistency.

"Nothing."

She looked up, expecting to see Roger was playing a joke on her, and this wasn't really the project he'd hired her for. But there was no hint of that. Turning her attention back to the photo, she tried to gather as much as she could from it. She wasn't a historian by any means, but it appeared to have been taken maybe around the time her great-grandparents were alive. Guessing wasn't something she was used to doing. She functioned on facts, and right now she had none. "I'm not sure I'm going to be much help."

"Why do you think that?" Roger asked.

"I thought you needed . . . something different. Something more like . . . research."

"That's what this is."

Maybe to others, but this seemed more along the line of an investigation, and nothing like anything she'd ever done before. Was she qualified to do that type of work? Absolutely not. Was she about to admit that to him? *Absolutely not.* If she backed out now, why would he recommend her to the Henderson family? Not that she needed to impress Roger, but she didn't want to make him question his offer. She could find work on her own, but having someone speak on her behalf with the Henderson family was more than she dreamed would happen. *I'm not screwing this up.*

"Do you have a deadline?" she asked.

He shook his head. "No. But my client would like this information as soon as possible. As I mentioned before, no one can know anything about this photo or that you're working for me. Is that understood?"

Roger's tone was firm and direct, unlike she'd heard from him before. The picture looked innocent enough, but the hairs on the back of her neck said otherwise. *God, I hope I don't regret this.*

"I gave you my word. The only one I'll speak to about it is you." Of course she wasn't sure she would actually learn anything.

"Good. Now, did you bring it?"

Roger changed subjects so fast she wasn't sure what he was speaking about. "What exactly is *it?*"

"Your résumé."

Gia reached into her purse, pulled out an envelope, and slid it across the table. "I can't tell you how much this means to me."

He didn't pick it up. Instead he said, "I believe you should deliver it."

"Did you want me to mail it?" she asked.

"No. I was thinking more like giving it to them at dinner tonight."

Okay, somewhere she'd lost track of what was going on. Things seemed to be getting a lot more complicated than they needed to be. But why should applying for a job be anything different? "We're having dinner with them?"

"In a sense. There's a fundraiser tonight, and I know for a fact they will be there."

"I thought you wanted me to start working on this photo, not crashing some event." Roger leaned back in his seat and was staring at her. His lack of response was unnerving. But she wasn't going to give in either. She'd come this far before meeting Roger, she'd be fine without his help. Yet the silence was driving her crazy. So she took back the control. "I'm working on your project, but that doesn't give you the right to dictate how I spend my nights."

37

Gia didn't miss the slight tensioning of his chiseled jawed before he replied, "You're positive you want to decline this request?"

"A request would imply that you asked."

Roger cocked a brow and said, "I thought you'd be more receptive to my assistance."

That only showed how little he knew about her. "There is a difference. I'd take the time to explain it to you, however I have a feeling it wouldn't do any good. You appear to be a man who takes charge and does things his way." *Or no way.*

Roger laughed softly. "Yes. I can be a controlling ass. But I'm result driven. You want that job?"

"Not at any price," she said flatly.

Roger nodded. "Good. Because if you're so easily persuaded, I don't want you working for me either."

"So this was a test?" Gia asked.

He shook his head. "No. I would like you to attend the event with me tonight. Mostly because they bore the shit out of me."

"Then why are you going?" She already knew it wasn't because he was obligated.

"This is . . . personal."

And you want to take me? She could ask what was personal about it, but there was another way to obtain that same information. She could accept his so called invitation.

"What time and what's the attire?" She didn't have any information, and even worse, she wasn't sure she had the right dress.

"Black tie," he said.

Gia was screwed. It was Saturday, and she didn't own anything formal. No way was she informing Mr. Fancy Pants of that. Purchasing one was out of the question. But she had a friend back home who was involved in the local theater.

People were donating stuff to them all the time. The last show Gia went to, she'd been in awe over the gowns. *Please have one in my size.*

She got up and said, "I better get going."

"I thought we were going to talk about the photo," Roger said.

Gia couldn't believe him. She had no problem setting him straight. "I'm not sure how much you know about women, but you can't ask someone to a black tie event and expect them to sit around sipping tea and talking. I need to get ready."

She could feel his eyes slowly roam from toe to head. "Red," he said.

"Excuse me?"

"Do you have a red dress?"

Gia wanted to burst out laughing and tell him she didn't have one in any color. Instead she shrugged. "Why?"

"You can pull off a bold color like that."

With her hands on her hips, she stated, "Although I appreciate the compliment, I do *not* need your guidance on what to wear. All I need is time to get ready. Where should I meet you?"

"I'll pick you up at eight. And before you argue, there is no way you're riding a bus to the Gold Crown Plaza."

"Eight o'clock it is." With that she rushed out of the café, already dialing Vickie.

"Hi Gia. Are you home for the weekend?"

It was funny that no matter how long she lived away from Maplesville, her family and friends always called Rhode Island her home. "Sorry Vickie, but I have plans. That's actually why I'm calling. If I promise to make you my maid of honor, will you do me a huge favor?"

Vickie screeched. "You're getting married?"

Gia laughed. "No. But if I was, you'll be my maid of honor."

Letting out a long exasperated sigh, Vickie added, "That wasn't very funny."

"I know, but I believe I owe you for that surprise party the last time I visited."

She could picture Vickie's overdramatic eye roll. "Really, you need to loosen up a little."

"Vickie, you know I don't sing." *And definitely not in public.* But what was she supposed to do when her best friend went through all the trouble to plan the party around singing karaoke.

"Okay, you win. So what is it you need?"

"A dress. I mean a gown. Oh hell, Vickie, you know I'm not good at this."

"Tell me about it. Your wardrobe is meant for the office. That's it."

"Normally that's all I need. But I'm attending a formal event."

"I'm sure I have something for you. How soon do you need it?" Vickie asked.

Clearing her throat, Gia prepared herself for the gasp that was surely going to follow. "The event's tonight."

"What! Tell me you're not serious."

"I am."

"Gia, you are so darn lucky I don't have any plans today. It's going to take me at least two hours to go through my assortment and pack them into the car. Then I have to drive there, do your hair and makeup, and—"

"All I need is a dress."

Vickie laughed. "So you believe. I need to know more about the event so I can pick the right one."

"I don't know anything about it."

"Who are you? Because my friend is so . . . predictable," Vickie questioned teasingly.

"He didn't tell me any more than—"

"He? You've been holding out on me. If you want that dress you better start spilling it."

Gia couldn't believe she let that slip. But the clock was ticking. "I can tell you all about it when you're here. So you're thinking three hours at the most?"

"Are you kidding me? It might be worth a ticket. I'll be here in less than two. And trust me, I'm not leaving until I hear about *everything.*"

Vickie ended the call, and Gia put the phone in her purse as she got onto the bus. Sadly, Vickie was much more excited about her going out tonight than she was. *And whatever you think it will be is more exciting than what it probably will be.*

Roger normally sent a check for these functions. He got that they needed to raise funds. But for most of the people there, it was about status and looking as though they gave a shit. It pissed him off that they believed money fixed everything.

He wasn't so ignorant to believe it wasn't needed. The families of the fallen DEA agents needed the support. But they also needed the fucking cover-up and drugs to stop. Some of the people donating were also suspected of being connected to the drug cartels. Playing nice with them at this event wasn't easy. But eventually, everyone would be taken down.

Part of him wanted to go back to the agency. It was where he belonged. Even now, knowing he was going to be close to some of the active agents, the flashbacks tortured him. He didn't care who the hell told him it wasn't his fault, it still felt like it had been. They never should've entered that house.

41

Not without knowing who was inside. But it was all about making the bust. The meth lab needed to be shut down. They had the warrant. What no one knew, or expected, was children were being held in the basement.

He replayed it over and over again. The agents shouted for the suspects to put their hands up. Instead one pulled out a sawed-off shotgun and killed one of the agents. Then all hell broke loose. One of the assailants leaped through a window, still armed. Roger exited the building after him. As he tackled him to the rough asphalt, the sound of the house exploding rumbled through him and shards of glass and wood flew all around. He rolled over, not letting go of his prisoner, to see the house engulfed in flames.

One of agents stumbled out of the door and collapsed on the steps. Roger rushed over and pulled him away from the burning house. He patted out the flames on his uniform and performed CPR until the ambulance arrived. Even as they took the agent away, Roger knew it was too late.

He was the only survivor on the team. But they were more than fellow agents. They had been family, and they trusted each other to have their backs. Over the years, Roger replayed that horrible day over and over again. What had they missed? They had raided more places than he could count, and things had never gone so bad.

As agents, they knew the risks. Drug dealers, guards, and cookers paid the price for the choices they made. But the children had been innocent in all of this. The oldest one had been seven. They never had a chance to live their lives, to make their own mistakes.

And we should've known they were there.

They had been watching that house for months, not days. People came and went all hours of the day and night. They were all adults.

No one had been able to determine how long those kids had been in there, but they were eventually identified as children of the assholes running that meth lab.

Roger had been put on administrative leave after that. They thought he needed time to heal. If he lived to be a hundred and fifty, it'd feel just as raw as it had that day.

That's why he was still sitting in the limo in front of Gia's apartment building. It was bad enough he was going to this event, why the hell was he going to subject her to it?

He could tell her it was so she could meet and mingle with the Henderson family in a neutral environment, but that wasn't true. It wasn't as though pulling out a résumé and handing it to one of them would ever be a wise thing to do. If anything, she'd look . . . *desperate.*

That's not how Roger viewed Gia. She wasn't attending this with him for some damn job. Not the way she challenged him every chance she got. So why did she agree? *Sure as hell wasn't my charm.*

But now he was curious. She wasn't as simple to read as he'd first thought. And it looked like there was only one way to learn why, and that was by going with her. Roger opened the limo door and climbed the stairs to her second floor apartment. He knocked once and the door opened immediately.

He had eyes and already knew she was a beautiful woman, but he wasn't expecting her to be . . . *gorgeous.* Roger had suggested red, but this emerald green gown hugged every curve and accented her eyes. Before he could tell her how she looked, Gia snapped at him.

"I was about to give up and change."

"That would've been a shame, because you look lovely."

Gia stopped and eyed him. Then huffed. "Don't try to get out of the fact that you kept me waiting up here for almost

43

fifteen minutes while you sat in that limo. These shoes might look great, but they are killers on my feet."

She moved her leg to show him her six inch heels, and her dress opened, the long thigh-high slit revealed a shapely bare leg. *Damn!*

"You seem . . . distracted. If you've changed your mind about going, just let me know."

Roger smiled. She was right, the event definitely wasn't where he wanted to be with her. "I'm not usually wrong, but I was this time."

"About what?" she asked.

He placed a hand on the curve of her back as they walked to the limo. "Your color is definitely green."

"Thank you," she replied softly.

The ride to Gold Crown Plaza was filled with small talk. He'd rather have ridden in silence. He wanted to learn something real about her, but then again, he had alternate ways to obtain that information. And it would probably be more accurate.

Once inside, he made sure to stay close to Gia as there were several onlookers he wanted to keep away from Gia. Their reputations were well known. They wouldn't appreciate Gia for who she was. They'd see one thing, a hot sexy piece of ass, and nothing more.

Thinking like this was unusual for him. Not that he normally dated dumb women, but they were easier. Wine, dine, and bed. Deep conversations were never required, or desired. Gia probably wasn't joking about changing out of that dress.

"I didn't know you were coming tonight," Lena greeted them. Then her eyes widened. "You're the woman from the other day."

"I am," Gia smiled. "Thank you again for the ride home. It was so much easier."

"Are you kidding me? If I hadn't had a doctor's appointment to check on this little one, I'd have gone along with you." Lena rubbed her well-rounded belly. "I'm wondering if three is the magic number."

Brice joined them and added, "I'm thinking it's four."

Lena gave him a playful elbow to the ribs. "Let me have this one before you start thinking about the next. What do you think?" Lena asked Gia.

Gia laughed. "I'm an only child, and I don't have any children."

Lena snickered. "Oh, then you'll have six for sure. I don't think we ever formally introduced ourselves the other day. I'm Lena, and this is my husband Brice."

"So nice to meet you both. I'm Gia Gravel."

Lena peered at Roger and said, "I thought you said you weren't coming?"

"I changed my mind," he replied.

Lena gave him a wink and said, "I can see why. But I didn't realize you two knew each other. I feel foolish now about insisting my driver give you a lift home."

"Not at all. I really appreciated it," Gia replied. She looked at him, and he knew she was going along as planned. "Drenched rat isn't my best look," Gia added, chuckling softly.

"I hope that little mishap didn't interfere in any lunch plans you two may have had."

Roger didn't want Gia answering this. It was the perfect time for him to interject. "Actually, Gia wasn't there to see me. She was there to drop off her résumé." Placing a hand on Gia's back, he added, "Until now, I don't believe you even knew I was friends with the Hendersons, did you?"

Gia shook her head. "No, I didn't. Maybe I shouldn't apply then."

Brice chimed in, "We won't hold it against you."

Roger noticed Lena give Brice an elbow to the ribs. "You don't want to scare her away."

"You mean from working for us?" Brice asked.

Lena rolled her eyes. "Really? How is it these two men run successful businesses?"

Roger and Brice asked in unison, "What does that mean?"

Lena shook her head and ignored their question. "That dress is lovely. I wish I could wear something like that. I'd look like a giant pea right now."

Gia smiled. "Thank you."

"If you're not busy tomorrow, would you like to meet for lunch?"

"That would be nice," Gia replied.

Lena said, "How about we meet at Henderson Towers at noon? And bring that résumé with you. We can drop it off at Human Resources before we eat."

Roger could feel Gia's body tense in excitement, even though her voice didn't show a hint. "That's very sweet of you, Lena."

"I'm not so sure about that. I'm craving spicy food lately. How do you feel about Thai?"

"Love it. However, what do you mean by spicy? Give you the sniffles or sweat-your-head-off hot?" Gia asked.

Lena snickered. "If you ask me, I'd say just hot. Ask my husband and he'd tell you otherwise."

Brice huffed. "I suggest you don't try whatever she orders. Not if you value your stomach."

"It's not that hot."

"No. The sun is still hotter," Brice teased.

Roger was glad to see how well Gia was getting along

with Lena. That was good. Gia was going to be in good hands even after his project was complete. *Hell, she might never get to it at this rate.* There was no doubt that Lena was going to find something for Gia to do at Henderson Towers.

That was all good. After all, he only offered her the project to help her out. He really didn't need or want her assistance. So why wasn't he thrilled about this development? He wasn't going to waste time worrying about it. Brice hired him for a job. Roger wanted to complete it and move on. He wasn't staying in Boston any longer than he needed to. Hell, there was no damn good reason he was still there now.

"If you two will excuse us, I see someone I need to speak to," Roger said as he ushered Gia away.

She said quickly, "I'll see you tomorrow at noon." Once they were out of ear shot, Gia said, "I'm confused. I thought you brought me here to mingle with them and now you're . . . rushing me off."

"I kept my end of the bargain. You met and now you have plans."

"True, but you seemed . . . frustrated. Was it something I said? I guess I shouldn't have let them believe we were—"

"Gia, you did fine." *Too good and that's the problem.*

"Then what's wrong?"

He wasn't going to pretend he wasn't enjoying the feel of her soft flesh against his hand as they made their way through the crowd. "I saw an old . . . friend."

"I thought that was just an excuse."

It was. The fact she had picked up on it didn't please him either. But this event was filled with people he knew. Some he'd been hoping to avoid. As Director Larry Chamblee caught a glimpse of him, he knew he had to make the first move. He extended a hand to greet him. "Director." Then he

47

turned to his wife. "Mrs. Chamblee, it's nice to see you again."

"Roger. I'm surprised to see you here. And who is the lovely woman with you?"

Roger said, "Gia Gravel, may I introduce you to Mrs. Chamblee. She bakes the best apple pie you'll ever taste." He didn't want to get into how he knew them. The less Gia knew about him the better. *Hell, I don't let anyone know my shit.*

"Very nice to meet you," Gia replied.

"Well, I don't have to worry you're curled up in a hole somewhere anymore," she said, giving him a wink. "Looks like you are doing . . . well."

"I am," he said. "It looks like another successful event."

"Yes, but I'm getting too busy for being in charge of pulling them together. Did you hear we have two grandchildren now?"

Roger hadn't. Not because he couldn't keep up to date with things, but because he'd left behind anything to do with his past. That didn't mean he didn't support those who needed it. Keeping on the positive topic he said, "How can that be possible? It seems like you were just twenty-nine."

She laughed. "I've been twenty-nine for thirty-one years. And Larry is turning sixty-five. Hopefully that means he's retiring this year."

Roger looked Larry in the eyes and could tell that wasn't happening any time soon. The only way he was stepping down as Director of the DEA would be if it was forced upon him.

"I don't know about that. He's never been good at playing golf or fishing," Roger joked.

Larry nodded. "I see your sarcastic wit hasn't changed. But I agree with my wife; it's nice to see you here. Although I didn't see you on the guest list."

"You know me. I always have a favor or two I can call in." That's exactly what Roger had done. This event was by invitation only. Since he had always declined, they stopped inviting him a few years back.

"Although we would like to stay and catch up, we were about to head to the podium. It's time to acknowledge our benefactors. In the meantime, why don't you say hello to some of the other members of your old team."

You mean the ones who weren't killed. A few had been on vacation, and one had been on leave, spending time with his newborn son. Every time he looked them in the eye, he felt guilty for surviving when the others hadn't. Not that he wanted to die, but he didn't need the reminder that the only reason he was alive, was because some piece of shit had decided to make a run for it.

"Maybe another time." He pulled Gia closer to him. "I promised Gia a dance."

Her green eyes widened, but she smiled at him and replied, "And you're not getting out of it either."

As they walked to dance floor, Roger wished he'd come up with something not so physical, but it worked. Mrs. Chamblee seemed tickled to see how he and Gia connected. It was funny, because she had forgotten that, as a DEA agent, Roger had done more undercover work than he could recall and acting was a required skill. Gia, on the other hand, didn't know that.

The music was already playing, and she said, "I think you're supposed to put your arms around me and smile if you want them to believe it."

He looked at her and did as she said, pulling her so close he could feel her firm breasts pressed against him through his tuxedo jacket. As they moved to the rhythm, he said, "I'm not sure what a compliance auditor actually does, but you're full of surprises."

"I research information. And that's what I did about this fundraiser." She grinned at him and asked, "Did you really think I was going to attend, knowing it was black tie?"

"I had hoped so."

"While my friend Vickie was over, we did some digging. It really wasn't difficult, only one thing was taking place at Gold Crown Plaza. I take it Director Chamblee is your boss?"

He glared at her. Roger didn't like his life being looked into, even by her. "Former boss. I work for myself now."

"So you were DEA before?"

"I was." There was no point denying it.

"Why did you leave?" Gia asked.

Looking into her eyes, he stopped dancing and said, "You're hired to find out who is in the photo, not to get to know me better."

"Or at all," Gia said. He nodded. "Well then, I guess I don't feel like dancing any longer. Should we try the appetizers or mingle some more?"

He wasn't about to let her go. "I say we finish what we started." Pulling her back into his arms, he added, "Then after the dance, we eat."

Gia didn't resist but the rest of the evening was pleasantries only. He knew his lack of communication was as good as telling her he wasn't interested. She was spending the next day with Lena. There wasn't anything more Gia needed from him.

And the faster she's out of my hair, the better.

CHAPTER 4

"Not even a kiss goodnight? You've got to be kidding me," Vickie said. "What type of guy takes a woman out on a date like that and gives not even a peck on the cheek."

"Vickie, how many times do I need to tell you? It wasn't a date. He just needed a companion to attend the event." She still didn't understand why. It wasn't as though he was shy or insecure. And at no point did he *need* her for anything. Even this research project was questionable now. *Probably a picture of his family.*

"Gia, are you forgetting I was watching from your apartment window last night? Maybe you should try living a bit; quit looking for what's wrong and start seeing what's right. The guy is drop-dead gorgeous. There is no way he's struggling for a *companion*. I bet there are women lined up drooling over him."

That wasn't making her feel any better. "Vickie, I was only calling to say thank you for loaning me the dress. Not for a lecture."

"Why don't you take the train and I'll pick you up. We can spend the day together."

"So you can you can tell me in person what I don't want to hear over the phone?" Gia asked.

"That's not funny. We're best friends, and I only want you to be happy."

"I know, and if I didn't have plans, I might actually take you up on the invitation."

Vickie's tone was high-pitched. "You mean you're seeing him again today? I knew it."

With a sigh, Gia replied, "I'm meeting someone for lunch and also turning in my résumé to HR."

"Yeah right."

"Why would I lie?"

"You tell me. It's Sunday. Who is working in HR? No one, that's who," Vickie stated sarcastically.

Gia couldn't believe she hadn't thought of that. Lena seemed so sincere about helping her. Had she only been kind, hoping Gia wouldn't show? Nothing about Lena felt . . . fake.

"I'm sure there was a misunderstanding. We are supposed to do lunch today. Maybe HR is tomorrow or she's going to take it in herself." *Or it's going in the trash.* It was ridiculous to think one brief meeting was going to change her life forever.

"Gia, you don't need to do this. Why don't you just move back to Maplesville? You could save money and, in a few years, try the big city again."

Although they were friends, Vickie didn't understand how Gia felt any more than her family did. She didn't want to be in a small town. She wanted the challenges the city brought. Yes there were times it was too loud and crowded, but she was never bored. There was always something to do. Usually work related, but still, she was busy, and Gia loved that.

"Vickie, you know I can't go back there."

"Can't or don't want to?" Vickie asked.

"A little of both. But I promise, if this doesn't work out, I'll go home. Not for good, but until I can sort a few things out."

Vickie huffed. "That sucks."

"What does?"

"I have no idea if I'm supposed to wish you luck or not anymore. I miss having you close by."

"Vickie, you make it seem like I'm on the other side of the world instead of an hour or two away."

"Usually you're working. I was hoping since you lost your job we might get to spend some time together. You know, maybe take a trip to the beach and catch some rays. When I saw you yesterday, it looked like you haven't seen the sun in months."

"It's the brown hair. You're used to seeing me as a blonde." She had died it because her boss told her she'd be taken more seriously as a brunette. Now, she's regretting changing anything about herself for that jerk. "I'm thinking of changing it back."

"Please don't tell me you're going to do it yourself. Last time your hair turned orange."

Gia laughed. "That really didn't look good on me either. Okay. I will come see you soon and you can do my hair." When Vickie wasn't in a play, she worked as a licensed hair stylist. But she practiced in Maplesville. If she took her talents to Boston or New York, she'd make a boatload of money. *And she actually might get noticed and land a movie role.*

But like Gia, Vickie was pigheaded and didn't want to hear it. Thankfully they loved, respected, and encouraged each other in their choices.

"Do you think he'll still like you as a blonde?" Vickie teased.

"You're not funny. I told you, he took me on part-time until I find a job. So really I should be only one thing to him, and that is appreciative for what he's doing for me." Gia didn't want to overthink Roger's motive. She knew hers and that was all that mattered.

"Fine, I'll quit teasing you. But I'm warning you now, *when* the two of you hook up, I'm going to tell you I told you so."

Gia rolled her eyes. "Sorry, but you're going to be disappointed."

Vickie chuckled, "Not as much as you will be if I'm wrong."

She wasn't going down that path again. "Vickie, I need to go. I'll call you tomorrow."

"You better."

Gia ended the call and rushed to catch the bus. Roger knew her mode of transportation, but there was no need for Lena to. It might hinder her getting the job. She seemed so laid back, but she was married into one of the richest families in Boston. *And rode around in a limo.*

Sundays were a different schedule, but so many people took public transportation that there was always one going deep into the city. She hopped on the first one and knew she'd arrive prior to Lena. Or at least she hoped to. She was getting off a block before Henderson Towers. It was a clear sunny day so she should be able to make it that far without incident.

As she sat on the bus, Gia looked over her résumé one last time. There wasn't a lot to it. Hopefully that played in her favor. It showed longevity. Of course she wasn't sure how it was going to work as a business reference. *Please don't ask what happened.*

Gia also didn't want to say she was terminated due to inability to perform. *Damn, this sucks.* She wasn't sure what to say to Lena. This wasn't an interview where they weren't allowed to ask certain questions. This was an information lunch. She hadn't thought it through. Thankfully it hadn't dawned on her until now or she'd have been up pacing the floor all night.

Gia slipped the résumé back in her purse and got off the bus. She was dressed much more comfortably than last night, yet her feet were still complaining from those heels she'd worn. As she approached the building, she saw Lena getting out of the limo. She'd also dressed more relaxed in a yellow and white daisy sundress and white sneakers to match.

"Hi, just on time," she called out. "Don't mind my shoes. My ankles are swollen and no other shoes fit. You'd think I'd be used to it by the third one."

"I'm not pregnant and my feet are killing me. Why do we torture ourselves with those high heels?"

Lena laughed, "Because the guys like them. Of course that's also why we wear those damn uncomfortable bras as well. By the way Roger never took his eyes off you last night, I'd say it was all worth it."

Unlike with Vickie, she needed to keep up the façade with Lena. "My feet might debate that." She laughed.

"We'll make it quick then get right to the restaurant."

"It's Sunday, I doubt there will be anyone there today."

Lena laughed. "Normally I'd agree with you. But I know for a fact the manager is in today. Don't worry, it has nothing to do with you. Just good timing, I'd say."

"If you're sure, because we could—"

"Nonsense. We're here." As soon as they were inside the security guard greeted them.

"Mrs. Henderson, is everything alright?"

"We were heading to HR, but I'd like you to call down and see if Brittney can come up. Would you mind?"

55

"Not at all." He picked up the phone and a moment later he said, "She'll be right up. Can I get you anything while you wait?"

Gia wasn't sure if he recognized her from the last time she was there, but if he did, he didn't offer any apology for being so . . . harsh.

Lena said, "No, we won't be long, but thank you."

They didn't have a chance to sit down before the elevator doors opened and a woman dressed in jeans and a T-shirt came out. "Hi, Lena. I love that dress on you."

"I just wish I didn't look like a balloon."

Brittney laughed. "You forget what I looked like when I had the twins."

Twins. No thank you. Although her parents would be thrilled, Gia didn't even have a boyfriend, so a baby wasn't something she should think about. It was difficult enough in Boston on her own.

"I don't want to keep you, because I'm sure they are missing their mama. But I wanted to introduce you to Gia Gravel. She has her résumé with her, and I'd like it if you could review it and see if there is anything open you think would be appropriate for her."

Gia reached in her purse and pulled it out. Brittney quickly scanned it and said, "Compliance auditor?"

"Yes. I review documents, policies, and procedures, looking for inconsistencies. It requires knowing the difference between company polices and the letter of the law."

"I'd like to set up some time to sit with you later this week if that works for you," Brittney said.

"That'd be fine."

"Great, I'll be in touch."

"Thank you, Brittney. I know you'll find something for her," Lena said.

Gia didn't want Brittney to feel as though she *had* to hire her, but then again, if it got her foot in the door, maybe it wasn't a bad thing.

"I'm sure I will." Brittney waited as she and Lena left the building.

"Don't worry. We have a few openings, and I'm sure Brittney will be calling you soon."

"Only if you really need me," Gia said. She didn't want to be indebted to Lena any more than she wanted to be with Roger. This was supposed to be business. Normally she wouldn't be going to lunch with the owner's wife, but Roger encouraged them to spend time together. That was yet another question she had for him, and she was sure he, once again, would avoid answering.

"Gia, we take care of family and friends. Although we have not known Roger all that long, he is best friends with Brice's brother. That carries a lot of weight. And besides, Roger didn't accidently mention it, you know."

That was the only thing Gia was sure of. "It was very nice of him. Unnecessary, but still nice."

As they drove to the restaurant, Gia asked, "How did you and Roger meet?"

The same way you and I did. "Nothing all that exciting. He kind of left an impression one day on my way home from work. And here we are."

Lena leaned back and said, "That's how it happens sometimes. Brice and I met years ago when we were in college."

""You guys have been together a long time."

"We've been married for several years, but there was a gap in time, almost four years where Brice and I didn't even speak."

Gia could see that still bothered Lena. "Must have been tough."

"It was. He was a different man then. Our separating was for the best. I didn't know it at the time. I think if we had stayed together, things wouldn't be as good as they are now."

"I hear every couple faces rough times."

Lena smiled. "It's how you come through them that determines where you're going. Just remember that when it comes your turn with Roger."

"Is that a warning they are coming?" Gia asked, knowing darn well there was nothing real between them so no issue could creep up.

"We all hide things we don't share with anyone except . . . someone special. For me that is Brice and vice versa. I can tell Roger holds something inside, but what that is, none of us know."

"Not even his friend Caydan?" Gia asked.

Lena shook her head. "Which is why I asked you to lunch."

"Thank you, but you don't need to worry about me."

"I'm not. I'm worried about Roger. Brice tells me I should mind my own business, but that man is hurting. I know it. Even though it might be tempting to tell the stubborn, pigheaded man to take a walk, step back and exam why first."

Gia was thrown yet again. She really had only met Roger a few days ago. Surely she wasn't the one he was going to open up to. But she would respect Lena's request. "I'll keep that in mind."

The limo stopped at the restaurant and Lena said, "Oh by the way, Brice wasn't joking."

"About what?"

"I eat my food so hot lately I won't be surprised if it melts the fork."

Gia chuckled. "Good thing the chopsticks are made of bamboo."

She gave Lena a hand as they got out of the limo. "I might just have to do that. But boy, I hope my taste buds go back to normal after this little one is born. I never could eat like this before. The other two, I had a sweet tooth."

"Too bad I wasn't there for those, because I know a place that has the best cheesecake."

"There's always room for cheesecake."

And if I'm right, I'm going to need something sweet after this lunch.

"When are you going to tell me about the girl?" Caydan Pintino asked.

"There's nothing to tell."

"That's not what Lena told Allyson."

Even from the other side of the world, women seemed to stay up to date on gossip. "Was there something important you called me for?"

"I would think this was."

"Caydan, just because you bit the bullet and got married, don't think I'm following suit."

"Married? That serious?" Caydan joked.

"Fuck you. You know damn well what I meant. I'm not husband material." *Or boyfriend material for that matter.*

"And I was? Hell Roger, compared to me, you're normal."

Roger wanted to argue but instead said, "Neither of us are. Speaking of Allyson, how is she?"

"Hounding me to find out about Gia. And trust me, she won't leave me alone until I tell her something. Hell, I don't even care if it's true or not."

Roger shook his head. Allyson was going to see through whatever bullshit story Caydan told her, if he knew the truth. So keeping Caydan in the dark was the only way to continue to pull this off.

"Okay, I like her. I saw her one day on her way home from work, and I couldn't help but pull over." *And apologize for splashing her.*

"Fine, I'll make something up, but next time, don't make me have to hear it from my wife. And when I say hear it, I mean an hour of questions she damn well knows I have no answers to."

And yet you want me to get married. Yeah, I'm all set with that. "How are things in Tabiq? Any issues you need me to come and handle?"

"Would you be bringing Gia if I said yes?"

Asshole. "Okay, this has been a great chat. Let's not do it again."

Caydan was still laughing when Roger ended the call. He wasn't used to hearing his friend so . . . *happy.* The best thing that had happened to Caydan was Allyson coming into his life. Because of her, Caydan found out the Hendersons were his family before he crushed them. He hated to admit it, but Caydan would've self-destructed if Allyson hadn't been the voice of reason. *God knows he wasn't listening to me.*

If Gia and Allyson actually met, he was sure they would get along as well as Gia and Lena had. Then again, maybe he should keep them apart, at least until he finished what he was hired for.

He thought for sure he'd hear from Gia first thing in the morning, but there was nothing. It wasn't like she had already been given a job at the Towers. Maybe she wasn't as reliable as she had pretended to be. *Or she looked closer at me and didn't like what she found.* The latter made the most sense.

Roger could call her and ask, but fuck it, he didn't need her anyway. What difference did it make if she changed her mind? None. All she would be was a distraction. The faster he found the answer for Brice, the quicker his ass was out of there.

He couldn't focus, and it was pissing him off. Slamming the laptop closed, he got up and walked out of his hotel room. As he got into his car his phone rang. *Finally.*

"Good morning, or should I say, good afternoon?" He didn't try to hide his sarcasm.

"Sounds like someone got up on the wrong side of the bed," Gia said. "I would've thought you'd be happy to hear from me."

"I am."

"Oh, this is your happy voice? I guess I don't want to hear you pissed off. Anyway, that's not why I called."

"Why did you call?" he asked.

"I have been doing some research about the photo and found—"

"Where are you?" he snapped. Roger needed to make sure she wasn't with Lena or anywhere any Henderson might hear.

"Home, not that it's any of your business."

"I'm coming over."

"Wait! What? Why?" she blurted out.

"This project can only be discussed in person. I'll be there in ten."

He ended the call and threw the car in gear. Roger had no idea what the fuck was going on with him. The information wasn't so critical that it required him to rush over to retrieve it. No lives were at stake. Hell, he wasn't even sure why Brice wanted the information in the first place.

So this bullshit he was spilling was for one reason only. He wanted to see her. *Damn!*

It wasn't long before he was parked in front of her apartment building and climbing the stairs. When he got to her floor she opened the door, her hair a wild mass of curls, wearing glasses and a T-shirt so long he couldn't tell if she had shorts on or not.

"Don't look at me like that. This is how I dress when I work from home. You're lucky I'm not in my pajamas," Gia said as she let him inside.

No. You're lucky you're not. The desire to help her was still there, but shit, she was beautiful, and his physical attraction to her was becoming more difficult to hide. He could feel the tightness in his jeans. The only thing that sucked: it was due to a woman who had become off limits. She was going to get that job with the Hendersons and there wasn't a damn thing he could do about it. He didn't need to ask, he could already tell she wasn't a woman who could have meaningless fun.

But I'm not interested in anything serious.

When he stepped inside, he found her kitchen table filled with books. "I take it you like reading."

"These are research. Or did you forget you hired me to do some?" When Roger shook his head, she added, "You can obtain a lot of information on the internet, but sometimes you need to resort to print. It's easier. Would you like to sit down and hear what I learned?"

There was no sitting at the table; even the chairs were piled high. So he opted for the couch. She brought over the laptop and the photo he'd given her.

"So as I suspected, this picture wasn't taken any time recently. Not that you couldn't have figured that out. The time period is the easiest piece."

"Why is that?"

Gia handed him her laptop and said, "Wait, I forgot something." When she returned she held a magnifying glass. "Look closely at the paper. Do you see it?"

Even with the magnifier, he strained his eyes. "I can't make out what it says."

"November 11, 1918."

"The end of World War I."

"Yes, but that paper was printed in New York City. You now have a date and origin."

He couldn't stop staring at the picture. How was it both he and Brice had missed such a detail? Most likely because they were focused on the kids. "That . . . impressive."

"I just impressed myself out of a job." She laughed. "But you really went out of your way to get my résumé in front of the Hendersons, so I had to show you I wouldn't let you, or them, down."

I'm sure you wouldn't. "This is a good start. Did Lena actually give you a start date?"

"No. Their HR manager will be contacting me later this week to set something up. So we can talk. I don't have a job offer yet, but I'm hopeful."

"Trust me, you have a job." *Hopefully one you will want.* "In the meantime, what do you say about adding a little more to this project?"

"You mean who they are?" Gia asked. He nodded. "That's not going to be as easy."

"So you don't think you can do it?" Roger asked.

She looked shocked. "I never said that. I don't want you to think I'll be calling you tomorrow with their names."

"You're the one who set the bar so high," he teased. "But do what you can. I'll be working on some things myself. But I need you to understand something. Even when you get the job with the Hendersons, this can *never* be divulged. Understood?"

"I'm well aware of confidentiality. It falls under compliance. You have my word. And if that doesn't suffice, I suggest you find someone else."

He loved how feisty and defensive she was about her work ethics. He raised his hands. "I'll never question that again."

"Good. So if you'll excuse me, I have work to do."

"You don't have to start immediately. Why don't you have breakfast . . . I mean lunch with me instead?"

Gia grinned. "I meant clean up this mess and return the books to the library. But if you're free, I should be done by dinner."

Had she just asked him out? No. It was clear they rubbed each other the wrong way. But then again, they had seen each other with some sort of regularity lately. "What are you in the mood for?" That was a loaded question, one he was glad she wasn't asking him.

"Anything but Thai."

"How do you feel about lobster?" The smile on her face said enough. "Good. I'll pick you up at four. Dress casual. I know a place by the beach that is nice at night. If you'd like, we can take a walk afterward."

"With how much everyone is feeding me lately, it will be required whether I want to or not."

She walked him to the door and stood with one arm on it, looking at him with those damn sweet green eyes of hers. It took every ounce of control for him not to lean down and kiss her. He inhaled her scent, sweet like honey, then stepped away.

"See you at four." He walked out the door before he changed his mind.

When he got in the car he called Brice.

"If you're calling to ask about Gia, yes, we will find a job for her."

"Good, because you'd be a fool not to hire her. She's . . . good."

Brice laughed. "I'm not going to ask what you meant by that. Brittney told me her résumé was impressive. What does concern us is why she was let go. Any clue on that?"

"Yes, but I'm not sharing." *And she most likely won't either.* Whatever had transpired, Roger knew Gia was in the right. *And if I find out that piece of shit touched her, he's done.*

"Okay. I'll trust you on this one."

"That's not why I called. I have a question. What does New York mean to you?"

"Personally?" Brice asked.

"No. The photo was taken in New York City in 1918. Anything?"

"Like I told you before, we don't know much about our family. And even Bennett's digging didn't turn up anything. Just keep me posted on what you find."

"I'll let you know if I have any questions," Roger said and ended the call. He knew Brice was going to ask what or if Gia knew anything. He had no issue with lying to Brice, but would prefer to avoid it if possible.

The less anyone knows the better.

CHAPTER 5

Casual? As she looked at herself in the mirror, she wondered if she and Roger had the same opinion on what casual meant. If she was meeting up with Vickie, she'd have gone out in her T-shirt and shorts. But that wasn't appropriate for a date.

Was this a date? Roger's invites weren't really clear. This was a project he was supposedly paying her for. Somehow in her excitement of having something to do, they'd never discussed payment. It was possible each outing was exactly that: a thank you for a job well done.

Although she was enjoying them, they weren't going to pay her rent. Roger and Lena seemed sure she was getting the job, but she never counted on anything until she saw it in writing. And maybe the pay wouldn't be enough to cover her living expenses. She had learned to live without a lot, but rent, food, and utilities weren't luxuries.

Gia looked in the mirror one last time. He said he liked red, so her red tank top and white jeans were perfect. Casual, yet not a lay-around-the-house look. She took time to straighten her wild mass of curls but pulled it back into a ponytail because her blonde roots were beginning to show. *Good thing I promised Vickie I'd go back to being blonde.*

Although she really didn't have time to run down to Maplesville, she didn't want to meet with Brittney with a blonde streak down the middle of her head. *Looks like I will need to call in another favor.* Thankfully Vickie was between things and missed girl time as much as she did.

Gia grabbed her cell phone.

"Hi, Gia. Did you get the job?"

"Vickie, things like that take time. But . . . that's what I'm calling about."

"You know I'm horrible when it comes to mock interview questions," Vickie said.

"That's because favorite food or color is *never* one of them. And I don't need help with that."

"Fine. Do it your way. It's no fun."

"I'm thinking about doing it my way as a blonde again. Are you doing anything tomorrow?" Gia crossed her fingers.

"Would there be pizza and beer?" Vickie asked.

Gia laughed. "Afterward, yes. Because I don't want you distracted with all those chemicals on my head."

"Have I ever let you down? I mean doing your hair."

"Not once. So do you want me to come to Maplesville?"

"Normally I'd say yes. But since you promise pizza and beer, I'm coming to you."

"Why?" Gia asked.

"Because I know all the guys around here."

"So it's not really pizza you find better in Boston," Gia teased.

Vickie giggled. "I need to expand my horizons. And it seems to be working for you. By the way, have you heard from Mr. Handsome?"

"Mr. Who?"

67

"Don't pretend like you don't know who I'm talking about. But don't tell me now. Save the juicy details for tomorrow. I'll be there bright and early."

"Thanks for the warning," Gia grumbled. She knew when Vickie said bright and early she meant noon. Vickie never was a morning person, and Gia wasn't one to stay up late. How they stayed friends so long was beyond her. Maybe their differences made them fit so well.

Roger doesn't seem anything like me either, but I'm kind of enjoying his company too.

She had no idea when he popped back in her mind, but she didn't want Vickie picking up on it. If she did, Gia would never get her off the phone. The antique mantel clock chimed five times as she heard a knock on the door. The one time she wouldn't mind him being late, he wasn't.

"I've got to go; my—"

"Date is there?"

"You are ruthless, do you know that?" Gia asked.

"Absolutely. Have fun and remember *every* juicy detail." Vickie laughed wickedly as she ended the call.

Brat.

Gia slipped the phone into her purse and went to the door. She smiled when she saw that Roger did know casual. He was wearing a T-shirt that fit snuggly, showing off his muscular body with a pair of khaki shorts. If it wasn't for the fact they'd be traveling in a Maserati, it might actually feel like they were . . . compatible. Roger was way out of her class. She didn't know how rich he really was. Was he like Henderson rich? Either way, he was way out of her league, not that it really mattered, since she was working for him. *I think.*

"Good, you listened. I was worried you'd be wearing a dress or something."

"It may be hard to believe, but I am capable of following simple instructions," she said bitterly.

"That's not how I meant it, and I think you know that," Roger said with sincerity.

She nodded. Gia knew she was having some trust issues since what had happened at work. It was like she was waiting for another disappointment and building a wall around herself in preparation. That wasn't fair to Roger or to her.

"Sorry. It's been a long day."

"Then I think dinner is exactly what you need."

"Me too."

"You might want to grab a sweater. Although it's a nice night, it gets cool after dark."

She was up for about anything tonight. Gia just wanted to go out, relax, laugh, and enjoy. One thing Roger wasn't, was boring.

Grabbing her sweater, she followed him to his car. This time it wasn't the limo or his fancy Maserati. It was a Jeep with the top off. *Now we're talking.*

The restaurant was farther than she'd anticipated, but the ride was enjoyable. Roger took the scenic route, which reminded her so much of home. Funny how she loved living in the big city, but it never really felt like . . . *home.*

"You're very quiet," Roger said as they pulled up in front of the restaurant.

"I was enjoying the . . . fresh air."

"I don't know how you do it. The city isn't for me."

She turned to him and said, "Really? I would've thought that—"

"And you'd have been wrong. Put me near the ocean and I'm happy."

It was the first real thing Roger had said about who he was. "I'm not from the city either. I grew up in a very small town. One where you couldn't do anything without someone calling your parents and ratting you out."

Roger laughed as they got out of the Jeep. "I can't picture you raising hell as a child."

"Maybe that's why I'm a rule follower now. I got it all out of my system as a teenager."

"Oh, sounds like the topic for dinner." Roger winked.

"Only if you tell me your dirty little secrets in return."

She noticed his jaw flinch, but his tone seemed relaxed. "You might find I'm quite boring."

Oh, I doubt that.

They ordered lobster, and between dipping it in the melted butter and enjoying every sweet morsel, she shared some of her less colorful memories.

"I guess I judged you incorrectly, Miss Gravel. You were practically a juvenile delinquent. I wouldn't doubt if you actually got a B in behavior."

Gia snorted. "Okay, so I wasn't as bad as I make it seem. But I wasn't an angel either."

Roger laughed. "Not being home before the street lights turned on is far from being a felon."

"Does that mean you're not going to reciprocate?"

"On the same level? Sure." Roger leaned back in his chair as though in deep thought. Then a wicked grin crossed his gorgeous face as he declared, "I have a library book I never returned. And worse than that, they revoked my library privileges."

Gia laughed. "Good thing mine wasn't, otherwise we might not have figured out where that photo was taken."

"And now you know why I needed you," Roger said with a wink.

I don't think you need me at all. She was glad he pretended like he did, though.

. . .

"Are you ready for that walk I promised," Roger asked. He was tired of sharing her with other patrons. The beach was more . . . private.

"Sounds good."

Roger called the waitress over and whispered a request. She nodded and returned with a chilled bottle of wine and two glasses. He handed her a hundred dollar bill and turned back to Gia. "In case we get thirsty along the way."

"Too bad you didn't bring a blanket," Gia teased.

With the wine bottle and glasses in one hand, he reached into the back of the Jeep and pulled out a checkered blanket. "I believe in being prepared for anything."

Gia asked, "Should I be worried?"

"Only if the weatherman was right."

"Why?"

"He said it was going to rain tonight." They both looked up at the starry sky.

"But remember, this is New England," Gia responded.

"What does that mean?" Roger asked.

"It means wait five minutes and the weather will change."

Roger looked up again. Not a cloud in sight. "I'm willing to take the risk if you are."

Gia took the blanket from him and said, "A little rain never hurt anyone."

That's the spirit.

He led them over a rocky barrier and down to a secluded part of the beach. "This is it."

Gia opened the blanket and they sat down. Roger pulled out a Swiss army pocket knife and removed the cork. Pouring two glasses, he handed her one.

"What shall we toast to?" Gia asked.

Your beautiful eyes. Maybe your smile. Or that quirky laugh I love listening to. "Your new job?"

She shot him a warning look. "You know I haven't heard back yet."

"But I have. Spoke to Brice today, and he was as impressed as I was." More than likely it was for different reasons.

"That doesn't mean I have the job. Or if there is one available," she said firmly.

"Gia, if I wasn't positive, I wouldn't say it. I wouldn't set you up to be let down." That was why he was trying like hell to keep his distance with her. This was something casual. Not like they were hopping into bed or something. *Just wine and the stars. Nothing more.*

She either decided to believe him or stop arguing, but she raised her glass to his and said, "To the Hendersons."

That wasn't exactly the toast he meant, but he clicked his glass with hers. Roger never drank wine and would've preferred a cold beer. He was trying to give her what he thought she might enjoy. But she took a sip and by the wrinkle of her nose, she wasn't enjoying it either.

"Don't like red?" Roger asked.

"Sorry, don't like wine."

Roger reached out for her glass and put them both off in the sand away from them. "Me either."

"We still have the stars." Gia smiled.

"That we do." He lay down on the blanket and Gia did the same. He put an arm out so she could rest her head on it.

"If you're not from around here, how is it you know about this place?"

"I've traveled to Boston with Caydan so much over the past year, and I've had a lot of time to explore."

"You mean to escape from the city?" she asked.

"Exactly. Although I was invited, he needed time with his family."

"I'm confused. You seem to get along with them. Why didn't you want to go?"

If she was going to work for them, she'd learn this soon enough. "Caydan didn't grow up with his siblings. Actually he never knew he was related to them until last year."

"Then giving him some space was really kind of you. Too bad I didn't know you then. Maybe we could've—"

"The timing wouldn't have been good."

"Oh," she said softly.

"What I mean is, I was traveling a lot. Here for a few days, then back overseas."

"But with enough time to come all the way out here and find this place," she said.

"You're right." An awkward silence grew between them, and he knew it was his fault. "I guess I like my alone time."

"So why did you invite me?" Gia asked as they continued looking at the stars.

That was something he'd been trying to figure out himself. He could tell her she looked like she needed it. Or that it was a thank you for a job well done. This had nothing to do with helping her either. "I enjoy your company." It was the truth and all he would allow himself to admit.

He could feel her relax against him. "Good, because I hope you'll give me a ride back."

Roger laughed. "Do you really want to go back? This place has an amazing sunrise." He was joking however he could picture holding her all night under the stars. But he wouldn't want to stop with snuggling.

"Tempting, but I have things I need to do tomorrow, and your project is one of them."

The Hendersons might not intentionally be fucking up

things for him, but damn it, he wished he'd never agreed to do this. Just then a star shot across the sky. He didn't believe in wishing or hoping. Action was the only thing one could count on.

He rolled over and saw Gia's eyes were closed. "Sleeping?" he asked.

She shook her head. "Making a wish."

Figures. As he looked down at her, the urge to taste those sweet lips became too great. Leaning over, he brushed her lips with his. Her eyes fluttered open and she sucked in her breath. He pulled away slightly. "What were you wishing for?"

She smiled. "Not that, but maybe I should've been." Gia slipped her arm up around his neck, and he claimed her lips again.

He wasn't rushing this; Roger had been waiting to do this since the moment he pulled his car up. With the tip of his tongue he coaxed her to open to him. When she did, he sucked in her sweetness. Although he didn't like wine, it blended nicely with her. His hand ran up her leg and rested on her hip.

A bright light homed in on them and a deep voice boomed nearby. "Hey, you kids need to move it along," then added in a firm tone, "Wait, is that an open container of liquor?"

Roger saw the panic in Gia's eyes. *Yeah. So that bad girl type.* This only proved she was far more innocent than she let on. Roger rolled off her, sat up, and addressed the officer. "Yes, it is."

"You know it's illegal to have an open contain on a public beach."

Roger knew the officer was in the right. "I do. However, as you can see, the bottle is corked and we are not drinking." Roger also knew that where they were wasn't considered a public beach. The restaurant owned it, even though they allowed anyone to use it. If it came to that, he'd push the subject. As a former DEA agent, he wasn't going to sit back and get bagged for something that wasn't illegal. The waitress knew exactly where he was taking the bottle of wine when she sold it to him.

"Are you really going to argue the law with me?" the young officer asked.

Roger stood up, nice and slow, not wanting to aggravate the officer. "I'm not arguing; I'm stating. If you haven't noticed, the sign to the left shows that we are not on public property. If you have questions regarding what they do or don't allow on their section of the beach, I'm sure they would be happy to answer them for you. Ask for Jim. He's the owner."

The officer turned and appeared to look at the sign. The scowl on his face said he wasn't pleased with being proven incorrect. Roger wasn't trying to give him a blow to his ego. Then again, he wasn't taking a citation for something he hadn't done either. *There are many things I could've been charged with over the past few years. This isn't one of them.*

The two men glared at each other but eventually the young officer turned his attention to Gia, tipped his hat, and said, "Have a good evening, miss."

Roger noticed her sweet smile in return. "You too, officer."

As soon as the guy was gone Roger turned back to Gia who was laughing. "What's so funny?"

"I guess my wish did come true," she replied still giggling.

"You wanted a cop to come and harass us?"

Shaking her head, she answered, "Not exactly. I wanted a

night I wouldn't forget. Almost getting arrested surely fits that request. Just not as I imagined it."

Roger almost asked what she had imagined, but he could figure that out on his own. Kissing her, he could feel the fire building between them. Maybe it was a good thing that cop interrupted things. Otherwise tonight might not be ending with just a kiss. *And I'm not out to break her heart.*

"Hope that wasn't the highlight of the evening," Roger teased. Even in the moonlight, he could see her blush.

In her usual way, she deflected his question. "The lobster was amazing as well."

Since he was already standing, it might be a good time to call it a night and head back to Boston. "I don't know about you, but I could use something sweet." *But nothing will be sweeter than your lips were.*

"Ice cream sounds wonderful, but only if you allow me to pay."

Roger wasn't the type of man who let a woman pay his way. Then again, it was only ice cream. Was his own damn pride getting in the way? Probably. Instead he used what seemed to come very natural between them. Humor.

"Are we talking whipped cream?" Roger asked playfully.

As she folded the blanket Gia answered, "And chocolate jimmies."

Damn she's adorable. He wasn't sure if she knew it or not. Which only made it more intoxicating. "I hope you know I have no idea what a chocolate jimmy is."

She laughed. "Oh, it's a Rhode Island thing. I think the rest of the world calls them . . . sprinkles."

"Maybe you can expand my vocabulary over ice cream."

Gia smiled. "You have no idea what you're asking. We have a lot of . . . unusual sayings and words. We might need to order a super sundae to get through them."

I won't care if it takes all night.

Roger was in no rush for them to part ways. But after ice cream he was taking her home. And if it meant he stayed in the Jeep, he wasn't going to act on what his body was yearning for.

Damn, Brice better hire her soon, or I might just change my mind.

CHAPTER 6

"So he kissed you, right?" Vickie asked as she added more highlights to Gia's hair.

"I never said that," Gia stated firmly.

"You don't have to. I can see it in your eyes."

"Vickie, you're standing behind me."

With a chuckle she asked, "Do you really want to distract me while I'm doing your hair? I mean it's your head, but you already know that going from brunette back to blonde is a delicate process. So the best thing you can do is quit arguing and tell me what happened. Every *scrumptious* detail."

Gia rolled her eyes, knowing her friend wasn't joking. It wasn't as though anything crazy had happened, but since Gia had been living, for all intents and purposes, a dull life, she understood Vickie's interest. "Nothing happened. Well nothing crazy at least. But you're correct. He kissed me."

Sucking in her breath, Vickie shrieked, "I knew it! Tell me *everything.*"

Gia couldn't believe how dramatic Vickie was being over one kiss. *One amazing kiss.* "We were lying down on the blanket—"

"Here? Like on your bed?"

"Vickie, will you be quiet long enough for me to tell you? I told you, we went for a walk on the beach."

"Yes. Walking is vertical. Lying is horizontal. So skip the boring parts and get to the damn kiss already."

"It was nice. We were lying down star gazing. There was a shooting star and then he kissed me." It really had been very romantic. Like something she'd have read in a book or watched on TV.

"Like a brief peck or a, you know, *kiss?* The kind that makes your toes curl and your body tingle."

"Vickie, you read too many of those spicy books," Gia blurted out. *But there was definitely a tingle.* If that policeman had arrived a few minutes later, who knows what he would've walked into. She wasn't a reckless person, but with Roger, she found herself more of a . . . risk taker. She wasn't ready to admit to herself, never mind to Vickie, that she was beginning to like Roger. *I just wish he was easier to get to know.* Was time going to change that or was that just who he was? *Private or secretive?*

"Are you listening to me?"

"Of course I am." Gia tried to guess what Vickie may have said. Nothing. *Damn it.* "You said my hair is done, and we just have to wait for the color to set."

"You're right, but that's not what I said at all."

Gia turned around to face Vickie. Her arms were crossed as Gia asked, "What did you say again?"

"I said someone's knocking on your door." Shaking her head, Vickie added, "Don't worry, I'll get it."

Gia didn't get much company, but lately the postman had been putting her mail in the incorrect slot and her neighbor had been kind enough to deliver it. "This isn't Maplesville. Be sure to look through the peephole and ask who it is first."

Vickie looked through the hole, but said nothing. And when she opened the door, Gia's jaw dropped. She wanted to run into her room and hide, but it was too late.

"Hello, Mr. Handsome. Gia didn't tell me you were coming today."

Roger cocked a brow, giving Vickie the once over before he looked in Gia's direction. Then his expression really changed. "She wasn't expecting me."

Obviously. Gia hadn't looked in a mirror and didn't need to. She knew what she looked like. Her hair was plastered to her head with foils folded in it. Surely she wasn't the first woman he'd seen having her hair done. Trying not to look as though she wanted to crawl under a rock, she asked, "Did you need something?"

"I thought I'd take you out for a late lunch. But I can see you're preoccupied."

Vickie didn't give Gia a chance to speak. "If you want to sit and wait, I can have her ready in thirty minutes."

"Vickie, Mr. Patrick surely has better things to do than sit around until my hair is done," Gia stated.

Vickie boldly asked, "Do you?"

Gia rolled her eyes. *I really need new friends.*

Roger pulled up a seat across from her and said, "I'm free. My name is Roger by the way. And you are?"

"Vickie, Gia's best friend. Sorry about the Mr. Handsome. The way she described you, when you two first met, well that helped me come up with that nickname. By the way, I knew she had called it right when I saw you from the window."

The look in his eyes said he was enjoying this way too much. How she looked right now was no longer her greatest concern. How much would Vickie embarrass her in the next thirty minutes?

"Roger, I can meet you someplace when I'm finished

here," Gia offered, really hoping to put some distance between those two.

"Are you trying to get rid of me?" he challenged.

Duh. "Not at all. I was just thinking that"—*Think Gia* —"the smell of these chemicals might give you a headache." That was so freaking lame. There was nothing she could do other than ask him to leave, which would be extremely rude. So she had to suck it up and hope she could steer the conversation away from her.

"I'm sure it's safe, otherwise your friend wouldn't have put it on your head."

I don't know. I think she's trying to kill me by embarrassment. No one but Vickie knew so much about her. That also meant Vickie knew Gia didn't like her private life shared. Internally she crossed her fingers and tried having faith in her so-called best friend.

Vickie began chattering about Maplesville and how boring it was there. "And that's why I'm in Boston today. Well that and to work my magic on Gia." She shot Gia a brilliant smile then turned her attention back to poor Roger, who seemed cornered. "Which brings me to a very important question. Any single friends or brothers?" Vickie asked.

Roger shook his head. "Sorry, no."

"Figures. Gia had promised me pizza and beer after this. Guess I'll have to do that solo."

"You could always join us," Roger offered.

No she can't. Put a beer or two in Vickie and those lips would start flapping, then Gia was doomed for sure. Not only would Roger have a different opinion of her, he probably would call Brice and that once-in-a-lifetime job would be gone for good. Thankfully, Vickie didn't like being a third wheel. Not that lunch was going to be a date.

"I appreciate the offer, but I'm not sure how I'd meet

anyone with you there. You're handsome and everything, but you look intimidating. The last thing I need is someone scaring a guy off before I even get a chance to open my mouth."

Gia snorted, and Vickie gave her a warning look. "Vickie, I think that was the buzzer."

Vickie checked one of the foils. "Oh, this is going to look so good. Come to the sink and let me wash it out. Roger, no peeking until it's done."

"Vickie this isn't a—"

"Hush. I worked hard on this and want to see his face when he sees it for the first time."

Gia groaned, but there wasn't anything she could say. She had to get this out of her hair now or risk it being damaged. She followed Vickie into the other room. Once the door was shut she whispered, "Remind me to kill you later."

"You should be thanking me. If it wasn't for me, he might have left."

"And that would've been a bad thing?" Gia asked as Vickie washed out the bleach.

"From where I was standing, yes. He obviously is into you, just in case you didn't figure that out when he kissed you last night."

Even though the water was running, Gia didn't want Roger overhearing them. "Vickie, let's talk about this later."

"You mean after your date?"

The only way she was going to get Vickie to stop was to agree. "Yes. Is the bleach all out?"

"It is. Let's get you blow-dried."

Gia had a lot of hair so it took another ten minutes. But when Vickie was done, Gia was impressed with how natural it looked. *My old self.* Even though she loved it, it would take some time to get used to again. Time wasn't something she had.

Roger was sitting alone in her living room looking at God knows what. She didn't have anything inappropriate lying around. Those items were tucked away in her nightstand drawer. Hopefully, Roger was sitting on the couch, twiddling his thumbs. She knew she had taken one of those stupid "Are you compatible with your mate" tests in a magazine. Normally she left that sort of thing blank, but out of boredom and curiosity she'd filled it in. Roger may have been on her mind at the time. She had meant to toss it in the trash— mostly because she didn't like the answer. What the hell did some yes or no test prove? *Nothing.*

"If you want, I'll entertain Mr. Handsome for you while you put on some makeup."

She wasn't leaving those two alone for a second. Vickie would pump him for information or, worse, spill things about Gia she didn't need him to know. Things like how she had been the dorky nerd in school and the only reason she came out of her shell was having a friend like Vickie. Their differences complemented each other. She kept Vickie out of trouble, and Vickie showed her how to loosen up and have some fun. *I just don't need her planning the fun for me. Not with Roger at least.* Things were going fine all on their own. They didn't need nudging from a busybody.

But Vickie was on her way out the bedroom door, and Gia was forced to follow. When they got back into the living room, Gia was shocked to find it vacant. He'd said he didn't mind waiting. Then again, she had no idea why he would've wanted to. If she could've left, she would've.

"Well this blows," Vickie said as she collapsed on the couch. "All this work, and he's not here to see it."

And that's for the best. "Guess that means it's you and me for pizza."

Vickie smiled. "And beer. Oh, and you're buying."

"Of course. Are you ready to go?"

"You're not going out with me looking like that. Go put on the finishing touches so I'll feel like I have some serious competition out there," Vickie said teasingly.

Gia grabbed a pillow off the couch and threw it at Vickie before going back in her room. As she put on some mascara and lip gloss, Gia couldn't help but wonder why Roger had really stopped by. Pulling out her cell she sent him a text. IS EVERYTHING OKAY?

He replied: I WENT TO GRAB THE JEEP INSTEAD. BE BACK IN FIVE.

That was good news because she wanted to talk to him about the project. That didn't mean she didn't want him around for other reasons as well.

When she returned to the living room, she said, "Mr. Han —Roger, is on his way back. He needed to step out for a few minutes."

"Good. I was starting to like the guy, and if he blew you off for lunch, that might have changed."

Gia laughed. "I have a feeling it would take more than that."

"Not where you're concerned."

Vickie didn't have a malicious bone in her body, but she did speak her mind. "Have you decided to join us?"

"Heck no! There isn't going to be anything juicy to hear if I'm sitting in the middle. And yes, that's a hint. Step it up. Don't you dare let that man get away cause you're shy. If you like him, show him." Vickie gave her a quick hug and said, "Remember *show* not *tell*. Your analytical mind can't wrap itself around feelings."

"What exactly does that mean?"

"That you will probably trip yourself up or become tongue-tied. If you like him, put your hand on his thigh on the drive. Or reach over and let your fingers brush his so he knows you want to hold hands. I can't believe you're thirty-one and I still need to tell you how to do this."

"I know how to *please* a man." She wasn't a virgin. Gia had dated in the past. They just hadn't worked out. Mostly because she was focused on her career.

"I'm talking about what comes before that. You know, flirting. Batting those beautiful eyelashes at him and things like that."

"Vickie, I appreciate you doing my hair and lending me clothes, but really, I can manage this relationship myself."

Vickie smiled. "Finally."

"What?"

"You admitted it. You like the guy and called it a relationship. My work here is done."

Gia rolled her eyes and shook her head. *So glad you're not coming with us.* As Vickie headed out the door, Gia asked, "Are you coming back later?"

"Nope, but I'll be waiting for your call."

I'm sure you will.

Roger knew the ladies were occupied. Picking up the pizza and beer seemed the easiest thing to do. Of course he hadn't expected to find Vickie leaving when he pulled up.

"Perfect timing."

"Are you leaving?" Roger asked.

"My work here is done. Besides, you don't need me hanging around."

"Are you sure? I brought pizza and beer. Enough for all of

us." Not that he really wanted or needed her there, he just didn't want Vickie to feel as though she wasn't wanted. Whatever was going on between him and Gia was only a moment in time. She and Vickie had been friends for ages. Sometimes friends can be closer than family. A bond that shouldn't be interfered with. That reminded him of Caydan and hating that he was working for Brice behind Caydan's back. It was as stupid as being here at Gia's apartment now. What the hell was wrong with him?

"You look like you have a lot on your mind. Hopefully it's Gia. Enjoy your lunch. I'm sure we'll bump into each other again." Vickie gave him a slight wave of the hand as she headed down the street.

He stood there until she drove away in her baby blue Jetta. Even down the street, he could hear Vickie's music blaring. Never would he have put those two together as friends. Yet somehow, they complemented each other. *Gia probably is what keeps Vickie out of trouble.*

He grabbed the pizza and beer out of his Jeep and headed upstairs. He hoped Gia wasn't going to be disappointed that they weren't going out, but he was done with restaurants and crowds. He wanted a place they could talk freely.

When she opened the door, he almost dropped the pizza box on the floor. When he saw her last her hair was covered in foils and wet with some type of cream. Seeing her as a blonde, it was like looking at a different woman.

"What is this?" Gia asked as she grabbed the boxes of pizza from him.

"I thought it might be nice to stay in. Do you mind?" Roger asked, trying not to stare and failing miserably.

Gia wrinkled her nose. "You don't think it smells like a hair salon in here?"

"Right now all I smell is lunch," he said as he stepped

into her kitchen. That wasn't entirely true. Even her hair that normally smelled sweet, had a chemical odor. But the end result was . . . *wow*.

"What do you have in the bag?"

Roger smiled. "Since I struck out with wine last night, I thought beer might be better."

"You thought right. Vickie is an amazing stylist, but cleanup is not her strong suit. If you give me a few minutes, I'll get this place in order."

She put the pizza on the counter, and he watched as she began clearing the table and throwing things in the trash. He normally wouldn't go into someone's refrigerator without asking, but his sole thought was to help her. Quickly putting the beer inside to stay cold, he started helping her.

Gia stopped and said, "You don't need to do this. Just sit and relax."

"That's not my style. Besides, I don't want the pizza getting cold." He gave her a playful wink, and she handed him a paper towel and pointed to the kitchen table.

Unfortunately, he was like Vickie when it came to cleaning. He was usually in hotels and didn't need to worry about it, or home where he ate out most of the time. From what he could see, the only things out of place were somehow linked to having her hair done. Besides that, Gia seemed to like everything in order. That was in alignment with her career choice as well.

Gia wasn't her normal chatty self. It was as though when she set her mind to it, nothing stopped her. *She is a woman on a mission.* He knew better than to get in her way. In no time at all, everything was put away. When she turned her attention back to him, she was all smiles.

"Now about that beer," Gia said as she opened the fridge, took two out, and tossed him one. "Do you need a glass?"

"Definitely not," he replied, twisting off the cap. Gia had already set the table and pulled a pizza from the box. "I wasn't sure what you like, so I got a meat lover and a veggie lover."

Gia walked over and put the second pizza on the table as well. "I've never met a pizza I didn't like. It's one of my favorite foods. Guess I'm a cheap date."

Her eyes widened as though she wanted to take back her words. But it was too late; he heard her call it a date. Was that what these meetings were? Roger had been intentionally avoiding putting a label on them. That didn't mean it wasn't what they were. He replied, "Although I enjoyed our date last night, this is nice too."

Roger noticed the slight curl of her lips. She didn't want to acknowledge their changing relationship any more than he had. That was funny, because in his experience, women were always trying to put a label, or hell a ring, on a simple date or two. He'd mastered derailing all attempts. Yet here he was feeding into what he knew couldn't be. It wasn't just stupid, it was cruel too.

But somehow with Gia things were easier, which in a way made things a hell of a lot more complicated. How the hell was he going to be able to walk away from her without being an asshole? Really how she viewed him wasn't the most important thing. He wanted to know she would be okay. And why wouldn't she? Once she was working at Henderson Towers, she was going to be so busy she wouldn't have time to date anyway. The Hendersons demanded so much from their staff. At least that's how it was when he'd first started his research on them a few years back. Caydan said they'd changed. Roger wanted to believe that since he was asking them to hire Gia. He had a feeling she could handle herself, but the Hendersons weren't as easy to understand or deal with as most thought.

But he wasn't just going to up and walk out of her life. They had a connection of some sort and, even if they weren't seeing each other, he was sure they'd stay in contact if only through text messages. That is if she wanted to.

"I think New York holds the answers, and we go there to see what we can find out. Are you free tomorrow?" Gia asked.

While he was pondering whatever this was developing between them, Gia must have been thinking about work.

"I can be. What exactly do you think we'll accomplish there that can't be done from Boston?" It wasn't that he didn't want to go, but he had a feeling it wasn't going to be a day trip.

"I want to utilize their libraries. If I'm correct, there will be old census documents I might be able to use. But I can ask Vickie to go with me if you don't want to."

"Did I say no?" She shook her head. "And you think you can find this information that quickly?"

"I'm hoping. But I don't know. I went to college with a guy who is meeting me there."

Guy? There? "You're discussing this with others without talking to me first?"

"No. He just knows that I'm coming and have questions about researching a photo's origin. He's a photojournalist, so I thought he could point me in the right direction, if he couldn't provide anything else. What do you think?"

I think there's no way you're going to meet some guy in New York without me. "I can make flight arrangements and we can leave first thing in the morning." The look on her face said that didn't agree with her. "Would you rather leave later?"

"I don't . . . fly."

"At all?" Roger asked. She shook her head. "Afraid?" Gia nodded. "I'll be with you."

"It won't matter. I can't do it. I've booked flights before and gotten as far as standing in line to board, but each time I freak out." She dropped her eyes to the plate in front of her.

Since she couldn't meet his gaze, she wasn't only avoiding traveling with him. Usually people had a reason for such a strong reaction. "Did something happen?"

"My uncle was a fireman in New York City. He died when the towers collapsed. Even though I was young then, I can't forget the sight of the plane crashing into the second building and my mother screaming my uncle's name in panic."

"I'm so sorry." He understood loss all too well. Roger wasn't going to try to convince her it would be okay and nothing would happen to them, because it had nothing to do with that. It was a trigger for something she couldn't control. "We can drive."

She lifted her eyes and asked, "You'd really do that for me?"

He nodded. "It means leaving a lot earlier and, if you don't mind, staying a night or two in New York."

She was quiet, and he wasn't sure if that had been enough. Then she asked, "Could we take time to visit the memorial? I haven't been there since it was completed. I think it would make my parents happy." In a softer voice she added, "And make me happy."

He reached across the table and covered Gia's hand with his. "We can stay as long as you like."

"I promise I won't get distracted from why we're going."

"Gia, the photo is over a hundred years old already. It can wait a day or two."

"Roger, are you serious?"

"Of course I am." As far as he was concerned, this little project was ahead of schedule. Brice would get the information when he got it. If Brice didn't like that, too bad.

Gia turned her hand over so her fingers interlocked with his. "Roger, why are you so . . . nice to me? I mean from the moment your tires made contact with the puddle, you've been . . . I don't know . . . fixing everything. First helping me with my purse, then the job, and now . . . this. I wouldn't have expected this from you."

Roger cocked a brow. "I'm afraid to ask what you did expect."

Gia grinned. "Well, based on your looks and the vehicle you drive, I thought you might be a conceited jerk."

Roger laughed. "Then I guess it wasn't difficult to exceed your expectations."

"True," Gia teased. "But then again, I'm sure I am not what you expected either."

Definitely not. "You have surprised me on a few occasions. And before you start wondering if that is a good thing, let's just say few people can make me laugh." He stroked her hand with his thumb. "You've done that quite a bit."

"I didn't realize I was that funny."

There were a lot of things he could tell her he'd noticed, but this conversation had already gone deep and serious enough. "If I wasn't starving, I'd tell you more."

Gia grabbed a slice of veggie and another of meat lover. Turning one over, she made what looked like a pizza sandwich. As he stared she said, "Don't knock it till you try it."

Roger guzzled the remainder of his beer and then copied her technique. "I'll try anything once." He winked and as expected, she blushed. Although tempted to pursue this line of flirting, he brought the focus back onto her. "You seem to have had a busy morning."

Gia ran her hand through her long blonde hair. "Yeah. It was a long process. I never thought Vickie was going to show up so early either. I'm glad she did, or we'd still be stripping color from my hair."

"Stripping?"

"Oh you have no idea what it took for me to get back to my natural color."

Roger cocked a brow. She was a natural blonde. It suited her, bringing out her green eyes even more, if that was possible. "It was worth it."

Then Gia laughed. "I hope the Hendersons don't tell me to dye it back."

"Why would they?"

"My old boss didn't like the blonde. He said clients wouldn't think I'm capable of doing the job." She frowned and sighed at the memory.

"Idiot. A person should only be judged by their abilities. Is that why you quit?"

"Got fired. And no."

Roger wanted to know what the hell happened. She was honest enough to tell him she'd been fired. Would she open up to him regarding it all? "He must be a fool to have let you go."

"If he hadn't fired me, I'd have quit."

That spoke volumes. Softly and gently he prodded, "What did he do?" He knew he needed to keep his cool no matter what she said. That might be difficult because the look in Gia's eyes said she was still hurt by it.

"One of the clients crossed the line. The only thing my former boss did, or didn't do, was be in my corner. Instead he fired me for standing up for myself. So at the end of the day, it wasn't just the client who had no respect for me, my boss didn't either."

Between clenched teeth he asked, "Did he force himself on you?"

"He tried. I smacked him across the face."

Good girl. "What did he do?"

"Smacked me back and said I'd never work in this city again."

That fucking asshole. Roger needed to find out who he was. That bastard needed to be taught a lesson, one he'd never forget. He didn't want Gia to know what he was going to do. Instead Roger said, "And now you're going to work for one of the most prestigious companies, and not just in Boston."

"Until they catch wind of what I did to a client," Gia said somberly.

"Gia, that wasn't your fault. And the Henderson family wouldn't tolerate that either. They might be tough bastards in the business world, but I can assure you they respect and protect women. If either of them are stupid enough to come forth with that information and try to trash your reputation, it wouldn't be acceptable." *And their business would feel a wrath like they've never known.*

"You seem to know a lot about them."

"I do." More than they probably wished he did. And more than any of them realized too. "Trust me; you won't have that experience with them." Roger knew if anything did occur, even Caydan would have his back on this, family or not. Certain lines would never be crossed or other cheeks turned. *And she's one person I'm not going to let anyone fuck with.*

"If for one minute I thought they were, I wouldn't take the job, no matter how much money they offered me. My self-respect isn't for sale."

Gia continued to impress him. He was waiting to find something he didn't like or find attractive about her. Then again, she wasn't the issue in this relationship. He was. Roger could commit to a job or a project, but he'd never contemplated what it would be like after a year or two with the same woman. Usually he didn't want to know that much about them. The less he knew, the less involved he was. Yet he wanted to ask and learn more about Gia. It didn't matter what they talked about, he found her interesting. What he wasn't ready to do was reciprocate. Eventually he was going to have to share or she would grow tired of one-sided communication. *God knows I wouldn't have put up with it from day one, never mind for almost a week.*

"If you don't eat that pizza it's going to get cold," Gia said.

That had been her way of putting an end to the heavy topic. He picked up another piece and took a big bite. She got up and walked to the fridge. She returned with a fresh cold one for each of them.

"What do you like to do when you're not working?" he asked.

"Watch Hallmark movies," she said with a big grin.

"Shoot me," he said with a laugh. "There has to be something else." Gia looked as though she didn't know what to say. There was no way such a beautiful woman stayed cooped up in this small apartment when she wasn't working. "I mean if you were back home in Maplesville, what would you do?"

Her eyes brightened. "That's easy. When the weather is nice like today, I'd go hiking and exploring. Don't laugh, but I've always liked walking through the woods, off-trail, and searching for old artifacts. I've even found a few arrowheads."

Roger cocked a brow as he saw the light in her eyes as

she spoke about it. "Gia, do you like being a compliance auditor?"

Her cute little nose wrinkled as she said, "That's a leap from asking me what I like to do for fun."

"I know, but it's a serious question."

"I assumed that. Why are you asking it?" Gia questioned.

"When I handed you the photo, I could see the wheels begin turning. The excitement in your voice when you spoke about the arrowheads couldn't be missed either. If that is where your passion lies, in researching old things, why compliance? Seems so—"

"Boring?" she asked and he nodded.

"You don't have the same expression when you talk about it."

"I'm good at it."

"I'm good at a few things myself. Doesn't mean I want to do them as a career."

"Some of us don't have the luxury of doing what we *want* to do. We need to do what pays the bills."

Roger didn't know what it was like to go without. He'd grown up with money. What he hadn't had was a family around him. "Money isn't everything."

"No. But when you're worried about where the next meal is going to come from, it is. I was lucky. We always had food in the house and a roof over our heads. But my mother cut coupons and only bought what was on sale. Neither of my parents have a retirement fund. I worry about when they get older and can no longer work. I needed to make sure I have a secure job that not only will support me but will allow me to give back to them someday." Gia frowned. "Of course getting fired wasn't in my plan."

"I'm not one who believes in fate, but the timing couldn't have been better." *We wouldn't have met if you'd been at work.* "You're not working for that asshole any longer."

"Not working at all. I mean, besides your little project."

"Which we've never discussed your pay."

"You've taken me out to eat just about every day. I think that—"

"One has nothing to do with the other."

"How can it not?" Gia asked.

"I might not be a gentleman, but I don't ask a woman out and expect her to pay."

"But—"

"Two-thousand dollars."

Her eyes widened. "For what?"

"Work on the photo."

"I can't take any money from you."

He knew she needed it. So why refuse it? Roger could spot a person dealing drugs in a heartbeat. Yet understanding a woman's mind was another story all together. "When you hire someone, there's usually payment associated with it."

"I understand that. But it wouldn't be . . . proper taking money any longer."

Oh. The kiss. It wasn't as though they had sex or anything. But he could understand how someone like Gia would consider it crossing the line.

"So you know, this technically wasn't a formal job. It was more like—"

"Roger, no matter what you say, I'm not changing my mind. Consider this lending you a helping hand. Besides, it hasn't been that hard. Actually, it has been fun."

He could afford to hire someone to assist him. No one did something for nothing. He'd learned long ago, everyone had an agenda. Looking at Gia and those beautiful green eyes, he might have found the exception. She meant what she said.

Gia was a rarity. *A gem.* "That brings me back to the comment before."

"Which was what exactly?" Gia asked looking puzzled. "We seem to topic hop a lot. Even for me, it's getting hard to keep track, and details are my specialty."

He wasn't getting sidetracked. "Your research skills amaze me. That is what you should be doing."

In a soft tone she said, "Roger, I appreciate what you're trying to do, but I can't afford to live in a dream world."

If she wouldn't take any money from him for helping with the photo, there's no way in hell she would accept a job from him. Besides, he didn't have employees. What he did was best done alone. If he needed help, it wasn't the kind she could give him. *Unless she's a weapons expert and failed to mention it.* Nothing regarding Gia would surprise him. Then again, he probably wasn't what she thought either.

"What if it wasn't a dream?" She couldn't see the value she had to offer to a company through her research abilities. And if he was correct, Brice was going on her past work experience. He hated to do it, but he might need to intervene in her career path. *Why not open doors she never knew were there?* Roger prided himself on not being indebted to the Hendersons for a damn thing. Somehow that had changed since meeting Gia. *If she won't chase her dream, then it might have to chase her.*

She was quiet for a minute and then asked, "What time do you want to leave in the morning?"

"Gia, I'm serious."

"So am I. There are things I need to get ready."

Her tone said she was getting frustrated with the conversation. But why was she so resistant to talking about it? Pushing was an option, but doing so probably meant calling this an early night. He didn't want to leave her so early. *Hell, who am I fooling? I'd spend the night if I thought she wouldn't regret it in the morning.* But Roger knew she would.

"Is this your way of telling me you'd like me to leave?" If she was, he'd respect that. Not like it, but respect it.

"I don't . . . don't know." She sighed. "This is not at all what I expected when I met you. I never thought you'd . . . that I'd . . . see you so much."

Neither did I. "It was unexpected for me as well."

"So much has changed in the past week. I'm not used to it. Usually I have my day, heck my entire month, planned out. I live a very routine life. Or at least I did. Now . . . heck, I'm going to New York with you tomorrow. With no plan for where we will be staying or anything. This isn't me. Or at least, not usually."

It was becoming clearer to him. She was out of her comfort zone. It wasn't that she didn't like it, as much as it scared her. That's why she stayed in the compliance position. Taking a blind leap was breaking whatever rules she'd set up for herself. *And I'm one who doesn't follow any rule book but my own.*

"Maybe it's time to break a few of your rules." When he saw the panic in her eyes he said, "Or maybe just bend them a little. I'll make the hotel arrangements if that is okay, and you can plan what you'd like us to do while we're there. Is that acceptable?" Giving her control was the only way he knew she'd still agree to go.

"You might regret this."

I already know I'm going to. Raising his beer to his lips, he said, "Only one way to find out. It's late and the pizza is cold, but let's eat before the beer is warm."

She laughed. "Sounds like we have a plan."

There definitely were things in the works. Things she might not approve of. But since when did what people think about him matter? He was calling Brice when he left Gia's and set it all in motion. That smile he'd seen on her face was one he never wanted to see fade. *Hopefully she never finds out I'm the one who put it there.*

She was so adamant about not taking money that having a job created for her wasn't going to go over very well either. *What she doesn't know won't hurt her.* One thing Roger was very good at was covering his tracks.

CHAPTER 7

Gia had packed, unpacked, then repacked the same stuff over and over again. This wasn't a business trip, yet it wasn't a romantic getaway either. So she opted for casual attire and good walking shoes. Although Roger seemed to drive everywhere, that wasn't the best way to get around in big cities. You spent so much time sitting at traffic lights or in traffic jams. On foot you could easily maneuver around those obstacles and actually see something you wanted.

As they approached the city, she knew she'd planned appropriately. She was glad she wasn't behind the wheel, because vehicles were swerving in and out of the lanes.

"When was the last time you went to New York?" Roger asked.

She sat holding on to her seatbelt, white knuckled. "Would you believe I was sixteen and on a class trip?" That seemed like an eternity ago. "I wanted to see the museums, but Vickie wanted to go to a play. I'm sure you can guess who won that argument."

Roger laughed. "What play did you see?"

"I can't even remember. Is that weird?"

"No. Because it wasn't important to you, you flushed it out to make room for what was."

"I've never heard it put that way. Did you learn that in some psychology class?"

"Nope. Thought of that one all by myself. Impressive isn't it?" he joked.

Gia laughed. "Absolutely. Should I be concerned about what else I *flushed?* There's a lot of my childhood that wasn't important."

"Don't panic. Whatever you forgot, I'm sure Vickie will remind you. Maybe not exactly the way it happened, though."

Gia burst out laughing. "How is it you have Vickie pegged so easily and not me?"

Roger turned to her briefly, then back to the road. "You're complex."

"I'm not sure how to take that." Did he mean difficult in general or just difficult to read? *Maybe a little of both.*

He reached over with his right hand and covered her left one. "Gia, don't compare yourself to Vickie or anyone else. Trust me; you're amazing just as you are."

Roger was speaking words, but all she could think about was the hand now holding hers. It wasn't the first time, but these small intimate touches made her question what was really going on between them. Softly she asked, "You know this how?"

"It's my job."

She'd been wanting to learn more about him, and this seemed like as good of a time as any. "What exactly is it that you do?"

"I help people."

She waited a few seconds and realized that was it. *So you*

think. She'd opened up to him, and now it was time for him to do the same. "Is that what you do at the beach? Are you a lifeguard?"

"Lifeguard?"

"You said you lived near the beach. Since you're not very forthcoming, I thought I'd try guessing."

Roger laughed. "Not a lifeguard. I actually own a business that helps people who find themselves in situations they can't get out of."

"Lawyer?"

"No. There really isn't a job title."

"You could try describing it to me and I can come up with one for you," Gia said, smiling to herself.

After a moment Roger said, "I used to be an undercover agent for the DEA. When I left the agency, I wanted to continue helping people. Although I'm not working on drug related cases, I have gone undercover to help people."

She figured there was a good chance he'd been connected to the DEA when they attended the fundraiser last week. But how did the photo fit into that? Gia had a feeling if she asked that question their trip to New York would be cut short. Maybe she'd have some answers after meeting with her friend. *Or I'll have even more questions.* Roger had made it clear to not talk about the photo.

If this was all she was going to get about work, she'd try something else. He hadn't mentioned any family. Roger definitely had the advantage. What she hadn't told him, Vickie unfortunately had.

"I'm sure your family worries about you." She wasn't sure how smooth the transition was, but it was all she could come up with.

"There's just me," Roger replied flatly.

Gia prodded. "No parents or siblings?"

"My parents were killed in a helicopter crash when I was fourteen."

"Oh my God. I'm sorry." Now she felt horrible for asking. But the door was already opened. Stopping now wasn't going to change anything. It'd just leave her wondering. "You were so young. Did you end up in the system?" She had friends who had been raised in foster homes.

"No. I was away at a boarding school when it happened, and the estate continued to pay for it. I guess my parents knew if I had access to the money myself before age twenty-five, I'd probably have gone down a different path."

Like doing drugs instead of busting those bringing them into the States. "What made you join the DEA?"

Roger shook his head. "A close friend of mine at school had gone to a party. We all knew he smoked marijuana, but we never said anything. What no one expected was some bastard deciding to lace it with a hallucinogen." She felt his fingers tighten slightly on hers before he continued. "Unfortunately, instead of coming back to the dorm that night, he went to the roof of the science building and tried to prove he could fly. From that moment, I always spoke my mind. I guess the DEA gave me an outlet to deal with the pain of losing him."

What could she say? He'd lost his parents and his friend. He had told her before money wasn't everything. She now understood what he meant. She gave his hand a squeeze.

"It was a long time ago," Roger stated.

"They say time heals all wounds. For the record, that's bullshit. We deal, not heal."

Roger put on the directional and took the exit ramp off the highway. "Look who's getting all serious. And you accused me of taking a psychology course."

"Oh yeah, I did, didn't I?"

He nodded. "You're not so bad at it yourself."

"You're going to laugh if I tell you this."

"With you, there's a fifty-fifty chance you're correct on that."

Gia gave him a playful tap on his arm with her free hand. "I am a *very* serious person."

Roger grinned. "Or so you want the world to believe. You don't have me fooled."

There was a part that was true. She didn't let loose because she wanted to fit in with the dry, boring people she'd been working with. If she'd attempted to crack a joke there, her coworkers wouldn't have gotten it anyway. *Not sure they knew what laughing sounds like.*

"At least I'm a bit more reserved than Vickie," Gia responded.

Roger cocked a brow. "A bit? She's like shaking a bottle of soda pop. When you release the cap, watch out."

Gia burst out laughing. "You're so right. If she hadn't left when she did, you would've had my entire life story according to Vickie. Mind you, she's added a lot of color to the tale. My life hasn't been nearly as exciting as she makes it out to be."

"Oh I don't know about that. Remember, you told me there were those wild days when you were younger. A time or two you got a B in class or maybe forgot your homework."

"Or the time we were all caught skinny dipping."

Roger shot her a look. "You're really going to tell me that story now when traffic is so busy?"

"Of course. It's more fun this way." Gia smiled wickedly and said, "Maybe its best you don't know."

"You're pushing your luck. If you think I won't stop this car right here and wait until you tell me, you're mistaken."

She looked around and almost called his bluff. But all the vehicles blaring their horns at them would be nerve-wracking.

Gia would hold her ground when there wasn't such a negative effect for doing so.

"You win. Vickie and I were skipping school."

"You cut class?" Roger teased.

"It was bunk day at school, so everyone did it. Not everyone, but a lot of kids did." Roger shot her a look. "Okay, Vickie dragged me along with her. She was always getting me in some sort of trouble." *Those were the best times ever.* "Anyway, as I was saying, we skipped school. It was hot out and everyone was going to the lake. I'm not sure why I ever agreed to play truth, dare, or double dare with those people, but somehow I found myself having to skinny dip with Vickie and a few others. If you ask me, the boys rigged the game. No way we all lost."

Roger laughed. "If the boys made up the rules, then yeah, you were played. What I can't believe is you actually did it."

"Not only did we do it, but we had to climb to the top of a cliff and leap in. Thankfully we didn't have smartphones back then or I'm sure it would've been plastered all over social media." *And I'd never have gotten a compliance position.*

"Damn it!"

"What?" Gia asked.

"I was going to ask if there were any pictures." Gia sat, her mouth gapped open. "What I'd have given to be there."

"I'm sure you never would've tricked us girls into doing that."

Roger laughed. "Boys are boys. When we did it, it was winter and the girls had to make snow angels. So count yourself lucky."

Just the thought made a shiver run through her. "That's horrible."

"That's boys."

"And yet we still like you guys. We all must be crazy," Gia snickered. "Good thing you grow out of it."

"We never do. The rules just change."

Ain't that the truth?

Roger pulled the car up to the front of the library. "I'm almost tempted to drive around the block a few times to see what other little goodies you have to share with me."

Gia let go of his hand and unbuckled her seatbelt. "You're not getting all my dirty little secrets." *At least not all at once.* "Besides, I have an appointment, and I can't keep him waiting."

Roger said, "I really don't like you meeting him alone."

"He's not a stranger. Just a bit strange. And before you ask, no, he wasn't at the lake that day. He was one of the kids still in the classroom." With that she opened the door and got out. "I should be back out in an hour."

"I'll go check us into the hotel."

She nodded and watched as Roger drove away. It was funny, she didn't need him with her, but now that he was gone, she felt his absence.

Get over it, Gia. This isn't a vacation. He's not your boyfriend. He's a friend and you're here to help him get answers. With that, she went into the building in hopes of returning with some.

But even before she made it inside, her cell phone rang. There was no way he was checking on her already. When she looked at the caller ID it said *Henderson Towers*. Taking a deep breath, she answered.

"Hello, this is Gia."

"Hi, Gia. This is Brittney. We met on Sunday with Lena."

No way I could forget. "Yes, I remember. How are you?"

"I'm good, thanks. Upon reviewing your résumé, I see we

have a few positions you might be a candidate for. Could you come in this afternoon to meet with me?"

She rolled her eyes. Of course Brittney would call as soon as she arrived in New York. The timing couldn't have been worse. She didn't want to seem ungrateful, but even if she left right now, there was no way she'd make it back in time. "I'm actually in New York at the moment. Would it be possible to schedule for another day?"

Gia held her breath and waited. She could hear Brittney typing.

"I'm booked the rest of this week, but I can do Monday morning at eight. Would that work?"

"Yes, that's perfect. Thank you so much."

When the call ended, Gia exhaled. She was a wreck. She couldn't believe she almost blew a job offer because she was with Roger. But what could she do? She'd promised to help him with this. Asking him to turn around and rush back to Boston wasn't right. *Maybe it's the right thing to do, but it's not what I'm doing.* This was so unlike her. She prided herself on being responsible to the core. And she had totally forgotten about Brittney's promise to call her for an interview. What was wrong with her?

As she entered the library, she knew. With Roger things seemed to go haywire. She had scheduled this meeting thinking she'd take the red-eye bus from Boston and return that night. But now she was staying a few days. And for what? To see New York with Roger? No. She didn't care where she was. It was time with Roger she'd been looking forward to. New York was just an excuse.

After this little getaway, she needed to go back home and focus on herself. Not this photo and definitely not Roger. *Neither is what will secure my future. And that is what's important to me.* She'd never been unemployed, and she had been now for a week. She wasn't about to make it two. Not if she could help it. *I've come too far now to screw it up because I find a guy interesting.* Putting a label on it as anything more would only hurt in the long run. It was short lived and, as two mature adults, they both knew it.

When Gia texted him saying it was taking a bit longer than expected, he wasn't surprised. If she was meeting up with an old classmate, that meant getting through the good-old-days conversation first. Roger was good at blowing off small talk, but Gia wasn't. Maybe she missed home more than she let on.

He knew she enjoyed the big city, but he'd already figured out the traffic and constant noise wasn't appealing to her. For Gia, the city represented financial security. Her delay provided him the perfect opportunity to touch base with Brice and help that along.

"Roger, I stopped by your hotel on my way into the office today. I was surprised to learn from the front desk that you would be out for a few days. Did you forget what I asked you for?"

Brice was just as damn demanding as his brothers. None of that bothered him. He did things his way. If Brice didn't like it, he could find someone else.

"You need to know the results, not my every move," Roger replied.

"And do you have any?" Brice asked.

"I'll let you know in a few days. But I didn't call for that. I want to talk about Gia."

"Again? I already told you Brittney will be contacting her for a position."

"I know. But I think it'd be best if you could find something . . . not so mundane."

"She's a compliance specialist. What else do you want with that job?"

"Brice, don't go by her résumé. <u>I need you to find her something requiring research.</u>"

He laughed. "I'm a scientist, research and development is *my* job. <u>I can tell you she is not working in my lab.</u> I don't care how good of a friend you are to my brother. No one fucks with my lab."

Roger shook his head. "Not that kind of research. How about your brothers? Maybe Dean could use her?"

"He researches investment opportunities. Is that what she's looking to move into?"

No. Damn it. It seemed so cut and dry when he'd thought about it. Caydan was out. Logan was a surgeon, so he was off the list. Alex was a novelist; they create their own worlds. Shaun was a financial guy, just as fucking boring as compliance. At least to Roger anyway.

"Can't you create something that is not in the lab, yet still working for Hendersons?"

"It sounds like you have something in mind. What exactly does she want to do? From what she told Lena and Brittney she was open to anything that fit her skill set."

"I know what she said, but that's not what makes her happy."

"She told you that?" Brice asked. "Because the last thing I need is a person coming on board that really doesn't want to be here. I fire those types of people."

"Not in so many words. I just know what would suit her better."

Brice laughed. "Roger, let me give you some advice. A *woman* isn't one of your jobs. You can't fix them, mold them, or hell, change them. All you can do is love and accept them for who they are. If you try anything else, trust me, it will blow up in your face."

Slow the fuck down, Brice. Who said anything about love? All Roger was trying to do was help Gia find her dream job. "You're missing the point, Brice. I've gotten to know her and she's missing her calling."

"And *you're* missing mine. Roger, I've only known you for about a year, but I know enough to realize one thing. You like control. No different than I do or Caydan or a lot of others I won't mention. I can do as you ask and make up some job we don't have. But women *always* find out. I'm not sure how, but they do. Shit, if we could connect to what data source they have, we wouldn't get ourselves in so much trouble."

This wasn't getting him anywhere. It might not be the job he'd envisioned Gia doing for the rest of her life, but it would hold her until that one came up. Roger laughed to himself. *Hell, I'm starting to sound like her now.*

Turning the conversation, Roger said, "I'm hoping to have more information about who is in the picture within the next few days. Is that all you're going to want?"

"Guess that depends on what you find."

"Okay, I'll let you know." He ended the call as he saw Gia leaving the library and approaching the car. When she got in he said, "I thought they were going to lock you inside."

"I'm sorry. I never thought I'd spend the day there. If they weren't closing, I might still be sitting at the desk."

"Were you with your friend the entire time?" He was only asking because . . . hell, because he wanted to know. Six hours had passed. No way could a guy sit there and talk for that long. Not unless he was interested in her.

"No. He gave me the information I needed and showed me where I had to look. Then he went off to work, and I've had my nose in books since. I didn't even stop to eat because I was so focused."

Roger had no idea why that pleased him so much. It had nothing to do with the photo either. "Should we find someplace to eat, and you can tell me what you learned?"

She looked at him and asked, "I know this is going to sound like an odd request, but do you think we can go to the hotel and order room service?"

"Tired?"

"No. I don't think I want to discuss this in public."

She definitely piqued his interest. "The hotel it is."

Roger had booked them a suite with adjoining rooms, not that they were going to need it. Once inside they ordered their meal and went to sit down on the couch. She brought her laptop with her as well as a few books she must've borrowed from the library.

"Productive day I take it?"

She nodded. "Yes and no. I have news I'm not sure is good or bad."

"Might as well just spill it."

"Can I ask you a question first?"

Roger cocked a brow. "I'm not sure I'll be able to answer it."

"I understand. But are you doing this because the Hendersons asked you to or because you want to know?"

How was it that she'd put those two together? Answering that was going to be difficult. If he said for himself, would that mean she felt more comfortable sharing what she'd learned? Or was it the total opposite and she'd worry he was invading the privacy of her potential new employer. *Fuck. Which one?* He had no choice but to go with the truth.

"This was a personal favor for Brice. But *no one* can know about your involvement. Not even Brice."

"So he is the one looking for this information?"

"Yes."

"I'm confused," Gia stated.

"Maybe if you tell me what you learned, I can connect the dots for you." With the Hendersons, that wasn't always as easily done as said.

"What do you know about their grandmother?"

Roger shrugged. "She was divorced with one child, James. And she died when the other kids were young, so they don't know much about her either. Why?"

She pulled out the photo he'd given her and handed it to him. Then she pointed to the little girl holding the teddy bear. "This is her, Audrey."

He looked at the picture and asked, "Who is she with?"

"Her younger brother."

As far as he knew, Audrey didn't have any siblings. But something could've happened to him when he was young, and that's why no one ever knew of his existence.

"What's his name?" Roger asked.

"Charles Lawson. And you'll never guess where he spent most of his life."

"New York City."

Gia huffed. "Well that was a letdown. How do you know?"

"Because Charles Lawson was the owner of C. J. Lawson Steel. His company built half of this city. It was a family business. Charles's grandfather had started building the skyscrapers in the late 1800s and then his father continued and so on. Hell, it's still a family business."

"Let me guess, you're a history buff too."

"No. My parents were architects for that type of construction. Lawson was talked about a lot when I was growing up."

"So you knew him?" Gia asked.

"I'm forty-two, not a hundred and two."

Gia laughed. "I just thought you looked good for your age."

"Keep it up and I'll eat your burger too," he teased.

"I'm starving. It might not be a risk worth taking," she joked back. Then she returned to the business at hand. "Do you still have any of their old contacts?

"No. I wasn't interested in the business when they were alive. Even though they wanted me to follow in their footsteps, I didn't." The more they had pushed, the faster he'd run. "I knew a few names, but I never kept in contact with any of my parent's associates once they were gone." Gia stared at him for a moment as though she was going to continue questioning him about his past. He tapped the picture again. "Tell me more about what you learned."

"This is where it gets weird. No one ever spoke about Audrey. There was a rumor about her abusing Charles to the point he was hospitalized. Then from that point on, she was gone. Never seen in another photo, and never mentioned again."

"Then how do you know Audrey Henderson was Audrey Lawson? I mean, the Hendersons would've been able to put those facts together without any help."

"And that is why I do it old school. There was a newspaper article, just one, about finding a young girl wandering the streets. She didn't know her name or where she'd come from."

"There is no way the police or media back then didn't know she was Audrey Lawson. They were so well known in New York."

"Yes, but they weren't so well known in a small town in Massachusetts. All they knew was her first name because it was on a paper in her pocket. When no one claimed her as

113

theirs, she was placed in an orphanage. She lived there until she was sixteen. Then she left and went to work in a mill. I'm sure you know the rest of the story."

He did. Audrey married the owner of the mill after his wife had been found murdered. There had been an age difference, and it was questionable why they were together, but back then no one spoke their minds. Everything was hush-hush when it came to dealing with the rich and powerful.

"I still don't know how you know for sure this is the same girl," Roger said.

Gia turned her laptop around and showed him the scanned picture from the news article back in Massachusetts. "It was taken only days after the one we're researching. There is no question. That is the same girl."

He compared the two photos, and Gia was right. "You're correct."

"Yet no one claimed her. It's as if she'd been intentionally sent away."

There wasn't anyone alive as far as he knew who could tell them that. "I can't imagine Charles would've passed on that story to anyone. If he even knew. He was so young himself. Maybe six and she was maybe ten?"

"Audrey was eight," Gia said. "And here is the newspaper article about Charles being hospitalized." Gia shook her head. "She might have been eight, but she was a cruel child. Not only did she beat him with a baseball bat, but she tried setting the house on fire afterward. One of the nannies caught her in the act."

And that psycho raised a child? No wonder James Henderson was such a fucked-up individual. Caydan had filled him in on some of the things James had suffered at the hands of his mother. Roger was sure there was more no one knew about. That didn't, however, give James a free pass for all the cruelty he inflicted on the Tabiqian women and their children.

"What are you going to tell Brice?" Gia asked.

"Hell if I know. I'd like to have more proof than just newspaper clippings."

"You could get a DNA test done."

Roger laughed. "You want me to ask two very rich and power families for a sample of their DNA to prove they are long lost cousins? Hell, I'm not sure either one would want to know how that came about."

Gia reached over and touched his hand. "Roger, it was an ugly time. The war had taken a toll on a lot of people. But that's all in the past now. Brice must've had his reasons for asking you to look into this. You have to tell him," she said softly.

He nodded. "I know." The problem wasn't the Hendersons being related to the Lawsons. It was two families now having to live with what had been passed down through the generations. *And I just hope this sick behavior ended with James.*

"Do you want to head back tonight so you can talk to him about it tomorrow?" Gia offered.

There was a knock on the door and a voice said, "Room service." The woman came in, set the table, and left. Only then did Roger reply to her.

He smiled and said, "They have gone this long without knowing. What will a few more days do? Besides, I'm excited to find out what you have planned for our stay."

Gia giggled. "Then we better eat quickly, because we're going see the Empire State Building."

"I've seen pictures."

"No. From the tippy top."

He wasn't about to tell her that was one of the first places his parents had taken him when they wanted to show him New York. He'd been there, and most major cities, by the time he was ten. Not only had he visited them, his parents explained how they were all designed for success. That's why he hated the city. The building that people stood and admired for their unique design, only reminded him that his parents weren't alive any longer. And when people told him their memory lived on in the buildings they designed, Roger wanted to rip their tongues out. The buildings were made of cold steel. His parents had been warm and loving people. How dare anyone compare the two?

"You don't seem too excited about it," she said softly. "I told you you'd regret letting me plan it."

"It's fine. I was just thinking how beautiful it's going to be up there tonight. Not a cloud in the sky." He refused to let her know the pain it brought back, thinking about taking that elevator up.

"Think we'll see any shooting stars?"

He wasn't about to crush her dream. New York was so bright at night that no one could see stars. Instead he winked and said, "You don't have to wait that long if you want another kiss."

She tossed her linen napkin at him. "How dare you suggest I would plan a romantic trip to the top of the Empire State Building just to get one of your kisses?"

Leaning closer he whispered only inches from her lips, "Would you rather stay here and play truth, dare, or double dare? Because I'd dare you to kiss me right now."

Gia licked her lips, and he fought like hell to hold back. *Fuck it. It's just a game.* He claimed her lips. That at least got a moan out of her.

When he kissed her a second time, he felt her tongue lick his lips. Roger wasn't sure how far she was willing to go, but he wanted her. All of her. Pulling back slightly, he felt her arm reach up and wrap around his neck.

"Not yet. I'm enjoying this dream."

Roger pulled away a bit more. "If we don't stop now, you won't get that kiss on the Empire State Building."

Her eyes were heavy with desire as she looked up at him. With a wicked smile she said, "You're right. Besides, we have all night to dream."

Roger put more distance between them. *Not if you keep looking at me like that.* He picked up his burger and said, "Then we better eat so we can go. I'm looking forward to calling it an early evening."

Sweet dreams coming our way.

CHAPTER 8

It wasn't really a letdown. The view was spectacular. The only problem was, all the other spectators thought so too. Gia recalled a movie where a couple planned to meet at the top and the girl had waited until closing just to see him again but he didn't show. She had given up on getting that kiss and seeing her love again. But like any good romance, when all looked bleak the hero showed up and swept her off her feet.

But Roger was by her side the entire time. There wasn't a time when he wasn't so close she couldn't touch him.

"Are you enjoying yourself?" he asked.

She nodded. "It's more beautiful than I imagined, but . . ."

"But?"

Gia turned around and said, "I liked the beach better."

Roger smiled. "Me too. Are you ready to call it a night?"

"I am," she replied. Roger held her hand as they waited in line for the elevator to go back down.

"You look disappointed," Roger said.

"I guess when I planned it I thought it would be less crowded. I know people are all cuddled up and taking pictures while kissing, but that's not me."

"If you want romantic, you need to find someplace not on everyone's radar. Would you like a few suggestions?"

Although she could use the help, there was no way she was about to admit that. So she turned the tables and said, "So when you complained about watching Hallmark movies with me, you were just joking."

"Hell no!"

"But you just offered to plan something romantic with me."

"Trust me; I don't have a romantic bone in my body."

She looked up at him and smiled. "I think you do but you're afraid to let it out. The walk on the beach was pretty romantic. And the pizza and beer too."

"Okay, don't make me regret doing any of those things," he said flatly.

She snuggled up closer to him and added, "And the kiss on the couch. That was pretty romantic too."

When he looked down at her his eyes were dark, but not with anger. "Keep it up. All these people aren't going to be around when we get back to the hotel."

Letting her tongue slowly lick her top lip she said, "I know."

Just before they got in the elevator, Roger's phone rang. She watched as he checked the caller ID and answered. "Hey Caydan, everything all right?"

She couldn't make out what was being said, but the guy sounded upset. A few minutes later Roger added, "Caydan, I have told him a million times, I'm not interested in running a resort. Not now, not ever. There are enough of you guys. Take turns staying there. I'm not a Henderson."

The call lasted a few more minutes and when it ended, Roger didn't have the same playful relaxed look on his face. "Things not going well with your friend?"

They were almost at the bottom when Roger said, "There's a lot more going on than that resort. I'm not sure, but somehow I think he knows I'm working with Brice."

"I swear, I didn't say anything." Actually that was easy because she just found out today that Roger was helping Brice, and she had never met Caydan.

Roger must've sensed her concerns and said, "I know you didn't. I've been in Boston too long, and Caydan knows me well enough to suspect something is up."

"Why don't you tell him it's because of me?" The words were out of her mouth before she could stop them. *I'm getting as bad as Vickie.* "I mean you . . . you know . . . helping me find work."

Roger put his arm around her waist and pulled her into him. "You're brilliant, do you know that?"

Nope. Because if I had a brain in my head, I wouldn't be siding with you over the Hendersons. Although she wanted to work for them, everyone in Boston knew they weren't a family to mess with.

Instead of getting off the elevator, he said, "Let's go back up."

"Why?" she asked puzzled.

"A picture speaks a thousand words."

"I took a bunch on my phone. I'll send them to you."

"I'm talking about that kiss."

"Oh. You want them to think that we're—"

"Exactly. But if you don't want to, I'll understand."

The kiss was what she had wanted, had planned. But at no point had she been thinking of it as a cover-up. It would be easy to go along with what he suggested. No real harm done, right? It was a kiss. Not like they hadn't kissed before. Yet she couldn't bring herself to do it. It would make the other kisses feel cheap. Not special any longer.

"Roger, I want to help you, and I think you know that. I'm willing to let you use my name and say you're dating me. But I'm not going to kiss you to defuse some situation with your friend."

He looked at her, grabbed hold of her hand, and hustled her out of the building. She could feel the tension in his body. He was upset. That wasn't going to change the fact she was standing her ground. *I'm not for sale.*

When they were far enough from everyone Roger stopped and turned to face her. "I'm sorry. I cannot believe what an insensitive fucking asshole I just was. You have every reason in the world to demand I take you back to Boston tonight."

"You're not mad at me?" Gia asked.

"Hell no. I'm pissed off at myself. I got so damn caught up in this shit, shit that is not even mine to worry about, that I totally forgot about your feelings. I crossed the line, and I'm sorry."

Everything about him said he was sincere. She hadn't expected such an apology. It was nice. "Roger, thank you. That means a lot to me. But I don't want to go home. Not tonight at least." Stepping closer, she said, "I'm not opposed to the kiss, just the reason behind it."

He pulled her into his arms and said, "Then know that this one is for one reason only. Because I find you utterly irresistible."

The kiss started slow and gentle like the others but quickly changed. Roger kissed her hungrily, his tongue tracing her lips, his teeth nipping them. Her body begged for more. His lips left hers and kissed their way across her jaw to the curve of her neck. She could feel her pulse race. She whimpered softly, "Roger, please. I . . . you . . . please." Her hands dug into his biceps as she clung to him. "People are . . . watching."

He pulled his head up but didn't release her. "Gia, I meant what I said. I'll take you back to Boston tonight if you don't want this."

She let her hand slide down his arm and entwined her fingers with his. "We have a dream you promised to complete."

He kissed her forehead and said, "Honey, it's a dream neither of us are going to want to wake from."

At least not tonight. She had no idea where this was going or how long it was going to last, but she wasn't going to let this time slip through her fingers.

Good thing I packed some not so casual things. For once she was glad she'd listened to Vickie and purchased the red lace bra and panties. *Let's see if red really is your favorite color.*

The walk back to the hotel seemed to take forever, but there was something nice about walking the streets holding hands. It was late enough that the crowds had thinned. She even talked him into stopping for an ice cream on the way. He wasn't sure if it was to torture him or if she really wanted ice cream. It was difficult not watching her tongue curl as she took long licks. And when there was a drop on the corner of her lips, he wanted to claim it, tasting all of her sweetness.

But no. She didn't seem in any rush. He got it. It was a beautiful night, but his mind wasn't on the weather or window shopping. Gia didn't seem to have changed her mind, so he assumed she was trying to make a lasting memory.

He was tempted to scoop her up into his arms and carry her back to the hotel. But he'd already fucked up once tonight and she was sweet enough to forgive him. He wasn't going to go for broke.

As he opened the door to their suite, she said, "I can't believe how late it is. Guess they mean it, New York never sleeps."

"Like all big cities, it has good things and bad."

"Well tonight, I only want to remember the good things."

He closed the door behind them. "Anything in particular come to mind?"

Gia smiled at him, "Oh a few things, but I'm thinking the highlight of the night has yet to come." She brushed past him and said, "It's been a long day so if you don't mind, I'd like to freshen up."

He was left standing in the living room as she entered her bedroom and closed the door. His body reacted to her closeness. What was it going to be like when he actually touched her? Ran his hands all over her silky soft flesh? *Fuck. Stop thinking about it.*

Was it his imagination or had her bedroom door been left ajar? He walked over and pushed it gently, causing it to open wider. He had rules about entering a woman's bedroom. Never go in unless he was clearly invited. But looking at the floor, it was as though she'd left bread crumbs to lure him in. First her shirt and not far off, her jeans. Outside the bathroom door was a pair of red panties and hanging on the open bathroom doorknob was the matching red bra.

Gia, you are driving me crazy. Even though the invitation seemed obvious, he stopped at the bathroom door and knocked. She was already in the hot steaming shower when he heard her answer.

"There's room for two."

Roger quickly removed his clothes, opened the glass door, and stepped in behind her. *Damn she's beautiful.* Gia wasn't like those plastic women. She was curvy in all the right places. Stepping closer, he reached around her and grabbed the foamy sponge from her.

"Allow me," he said.

His hands glided over her as he washed her back, then dropped down to his knee and washed her legs as well as her sweet round ass and hips as he made his way back up. Then he reach around her again, his body now pressed against her backside, as he washed her front. The sponge dropped as his hands came up over her breasts. He didn't need it. His fingers gently rolled her taut nipples and she leaned into him. The water quickly washed away the soap. She turned toward him, and Roger bent his head and kissed her gently. It wasn't long before his lips found their way across her jaw, down her neck, and over her collarbone. He moaned against her. "Gia, I want to make love to you."

"Roger, I want you to," she moaned as he claimed her lips again. Slipping his hands around her bare back, he felt her quiver at his touch. He brought his hands down, cupped her ass, and lifted her high into his arms. Her legs wrapped around him, and he could feel her womanly flesh pressed against his abdomen. His cock was hard and throbbing, but he refused to give into his own needs. Gia wanted a night she'd never forget, and he was going to give her one. *Give us both one.*

"I want to feel your hands on me," Gia said breathlessly.

"What about my hands and my tongue?" He lifted her high into his arms and flicked one nipple with his tongue.

She arched her back and said, "I want it . . . all."

As he sucked her nipple, he mumbled, "You'll have all of me . . . in time."

Once his lips came in contact with her nipple, he felt her body quiver in unison with his.

"Roger." Her voice trembled with need. He ignored her

124

pleas and continued to flick with his tongue and nip with his teeth. "Roger," she pleaded again, her voice barely a whisper now.

Oh, God, I can't wait. I want her now. His own desire was building quickly, almost uncontrollably. Forcing himself to think only of her, he reached behind her and shut off the water. Then he lifted her into his arms and carried her to the bed.

Gia tugged at him trying to pull him down to her. "Roger, I want you so much it . . . almost hurts."

"You drive me wild, Gia," he said before claiming her sensual mouth. She was perfection. He could inhale her intox-icating scent—like sweet honey and flowers—and never grow tired of it. But her scent was only one part. Her body was teasing him beyond anything he'd ever wanted before. His cock was pressed firmly against her thigh as he rested himself on top of her. The look in her eyes enhanced his hunger for her. He rolled over onto his side and pulled her close, claiming her lips once again. *She tastes so sweet. I want to taste every inch of her.*

As he continued exploring her mouth, one hand came up to caress her breasts again. Her nipples hardened instantly at his touch. The need to have more of her was driving him mad. "Gia, your body feels so damn good against mine."

"Roger, you're killing me," she whimpered as he sucked her nipple.

"There's no rush, honey. I want to hear you scream out my name and forget yours," Roger said, nipping her other nipple. Her skin was like silk, and he couldn't take his hands off her.

"Roger, I need you now," Gia tried demanding, but he ignored it.

"Patience, honey," Roger said, his words muffled against her cool flesh.

Her moans grew deeper as he rolled one nipple between his fingers and continued sucking the other. "Please, Roger, I need . . ."

He didn't deny her. He moved one hand from her breast and reached between her legs, finding her swollen clit with this thumb. Her back arched, and she opened her legs wider for him.

Slowly, he circled it, bringing her higher. As her body trembled, he repositioned himself so his mouth was only inches away from her center, spreading her farther until he had full access. Her hands gripped the blanket as he slipped one finger inside her and pulled it back out. Again and again.

Breathlessly, Gia begged, "I want you. I can't . . ."

"You'll have me, but first I want to watch you come undone as you lose yourself to my touch," he said as his finger entered her again, and he continued to circle her clit. She cried out in pleasure. It was more than she'd ever experienced. He was giving, not taking.

Faster and deeper he entered her with his finger until her body began to jerk violently. He felt her body clench around his finger with her powerful release.

"Yes! God, Roger. Oh, yes! Oh, yes!"

Her cries filled the room, but Roger wasn't done. He realized he'd left his jeans in the bathroom. Kissing her briefly, he leaped off the bed and retrieved the condom from his wallet. He tore open the foil packet, sheathed himself, then settled himself between her legs.

She wrapped her arms around his neck and breathlessly said, "Thank you."

"For this?" he asked, once again letting his fingers stroke her clit. "Or for having a condom?"

Moaning and arching her back she said, "Both."

He'd been holding back, trying to go slow, but her beautiful full breasts pressed against him and the heat from her core on his fingers was sending him over the edge. Moving back to her lips, he kissed her hungrily one more time. Then dragging his lips from hers, he slowly kissed his way across her jaw to the curve of her neck, stopping to feel her racing pulse. *I haven't even begun.*

She whimpered softly, "Roger, please. I . . . you . . . please." Gia's hands dug into his biceps as she clung to him.

The fact she could barely catch her breath was driving him wild. He knew what she meant and what she wanted. His cock did as well. Each moan or plea made him harder with anticipation. He ached to be inside her. "Soon, honey."

Gia reached down, brushed his cock, and cupped his balls. His body tensed instantly, and he wanted to enter her right then. Their eyes never broke contact, and her tongue slowly traced her lips. She knew she was teasing the fuck out of him. He could only imagine how fucking incredible her lips would feel around his cock. But if they were, he'd explode. There would be no way he could hold back. And he wanted, no needed, to be inside of her.

"I want to . . . have all of you, Gia."

She pulled him down to her. "Roger, I can't wait any longer. I need you to touch me. I want to feel you inside of me."

Gia arched her back, offering herself to him. He could feel the heat and juices from her first climax as her legs opened and her soft wet flesh touched his hard, hot cock. *Fuck yeah.* He reached between them and gripped his cock, slowly stroking her between the folds.

"Oh, Roger," she said, moaning his name again and again.

No one had ever been so responsive to his touch. *How is it possible to need someone more than life itself?*

"I could touch and taste you forever." He plunged his tongue into her mouth wildly. She met him just as eagerly. Then he urged her legs apart. "Damn, you're so wet."

She opened unashamedly, giving him full access. It wasn't that he wasn't ready, but he wanted her to explode for him again. As he rubbed the head of his cock over and over again on her clit, she whimpered and trembled against him.

"I . . . need . . ." she cried, her voice barely a whisper.

He planned to explore every inch of her, but his body ached for only one part of her right then. He couldn't hold back any longer.

"Gia, I don't want to hurt you." His voice was deep, almost a growl, as he tried to control his own need. "I'll try to be gentle."

She opened her legs wider. "I need all of you, now." She guided him, raising her hips to take him inside her.

He couldn't stop if he wanted to. Grabbing her hips, he pulled her to him and thrust fully into her. She cried out, not in pain, but in pleasure. Roger waited until she adjusted to having him inside her. Then slowly he entered her again and again. The more she moaned in pleasure, the faster and harder he pumped. *Oh, God. His own body wanted to let go, but he held back.*

"God honey, you feel so damn good."

"Don't . . . stop. Please, Roger . . . I'm . . ." He felt her body begin to tense again as he continued. She was on the brink, and he wanted to take her over the edge again. He entered her harder, faster, until she cried out his name over and over again. "Roger! Roger! Roger!"

Once he felt her releasing, he plunged deeper inside her as his orgasm met hers, rocking him to the core. He rode the waves of pleasure with her, stronger and more powerful than he'd ever felt before.

When he was spent, Roger collapsed and rolled onto his back, bring her to rest on top of him. Her breath was coming in gasps, the same as his. It may have only been seconds, but it felt like forever before either of them could speak.

Roger reached up and rubbed her back with long strokes. "I didn't hurt you, did I?"

Gia shook her head. "The only pain is from it coming to an end."

Roger laughed. "The night is far from over."

She snuggled up closer to him. "What are you offering?"

He rolled over again, this time she was lying beneath him. "Although your shower is nice, my room has a Jacuzzi."

"That sounds good. Maybe we can save that for round number three," Gia said with a playful wink.

Roger didn't need any further encouragement. Claiming her lips again, his body eagerly recovered for round two.

He wasn't sure what tomorrow would bring, but tonight he planned on giving her as much of himself as he could. Because tonight might be all they'd ever have.

CHAPTER 9

She didn't want to move. Gia couldn't remember ever being so comfortable. Lying in Roger's warm arms was heavenly. Reluctantly, she untangled herself and slipped out from under the sheets. The cool air sent goosebumps over her naked body.

"Where are you going?" Roger mumbled, half asleep.

Gia fumbled in the dark. She heard her cell phone, but she had no idea where she'd left it. "My phone is ringing. I think I left it in my bedroom." She scurried across the cold floor and located it on her nightstand. Her heart was pounding because her phone never rang this early. She'd missed the call, but checked the caller ID. *Mom.*

She called her right back. "Hi, Mom. Is everything okay?"

"Oh, Gia." She heard the tears in her mother's voice and her stomach dropped. "Your father had a heart attack. They're rushing him to the hospital now."

"Dad," she whispered, gripping the phone tightly. Knowing she needed to be strong for her mother, she asked, "Is anyone there to take you to the hospital?"

130

"Yes. We're going now." Her mother sniffled. "But you should come too. He was . . . unconscious when the ambulance took him."

Gia hoped her voice was steady when she asked, "What hospital are they taking him to?"

"RI General. Please, Gia," her mother pressed, "I need you home."

Nothing could keep her from her family. "I'm coming, Mom."

As soon as her mother ended the call, Gia rushed back to Roger's bedroom and flipped on the light switch.

"Roger," she uttered urgently as she sat at the edge of the bed, "I need to leave."

He sat up, squinting at the bright light. "What's wrong?"

"My father is being rushed to the hospital," she explained. "It's his heart. I have to go right now. Can you drive me, please?"

Roger was out of the bed and pulling on clothes. "Is the hospital in Rhode Island?"

"Yes," she confirmed as she ran back to her room to find some clothes herself. Since she hadn't unpacked, it was easy enough to do. Gia reached down and picked up the clothes she'd worn yesterday. Not ideal, but practical.

As she finished dressing, Roger joined her. "I know someone. We'll get a helicopter to fly back. Considering the circumstances, he won't mind."

She looked up at him. "I told you, I don't fly."

Roger walked over to her and placed his hands on her shoulders. "Honey, it's a four-hour drive or a one-hour flight." He gave her a comforting squeeze. "You're not going to be alone. I'm going to be right beside you the entire time."

It made sense to take him up on the offer. But getting in the helicopter wasn't going to be easy. She was an emotional wreck already, thinking about her dad. The stress of the flight might be too much.

"Roger, I'm not sure I can do it . . ." Her voice trembled as she said it.

He tipped her chin up to look him in the eyes. "I know you can. Let me make the call. We can be in the air in thirty minutes." She stared at him, not sure what to do or say. "Trust me, Gia. I'd never let anything happen to you."

She wanted to remind him they'd be hundreds—no, *thousands*—of feet up in the air. He couldn't guarantee his safety, let alone hers. But this wasn't about her. She needed to get to the hospital as quick as possible. Not trusting herself to speak, she nodded her approval.

Roger rushed out of the room to get his phone, she suspected, which left her with a few minutes to finish getting ready. She grabbed her toiletries and freshened up a bit. By the time Roger returned, she was set to go.

"Is this ready?" he asked, pointing at the suitcase.

"Yes." When he went to pick it up, she grabbed hold of his arm. "Thank you for doing this."

He nodded. "I told you; I'm here for you." Roger picked up her bag and said, "The helicopter should be here any minute. I suggest we get going."

Her stomach dropped. *Did he just say . . .* "Here?"

"Yes. There is a helipad on the roof."

"How efficient . . ." Gia said as she followed him. "Did I mention I'm also not a fan of heights?"

"No. But that surprises me since you took me to the top of the Empire State Building."

She laughed. "But that was different. I was trying to get a kiss."

As she and Roger rode the elevator, he said, "I'll kiss you the entire way back to Rhode Island if you need me to."

She appreciated his effort to lighten the mood. If she'd been alone in New York when she'd received that call . . . Well, she had no idea what she would've done. Roger was, once again, taking care of her, of everything. Gia had never considered herself to be a needy person. Or maybe it was because she never let anyone in close enough to help. Either way, she was glad he was there.

Gia was about to tell him it wouldn't be necessary, but when the doors to the roof opened and she saw the helicopter, her heart started racing. Roger was a step in front of her with the luggage so he couldn't see her panic. That was a good thing. She couldn't rely on him to be there every step of the way. She was thirty-one years old, for goodness sake.

Forcing her feet to move, she made her way to the helicopter steps. "Mr. Patrick," the pilot greeted Roger. "it's been a long time. Good to see you again."

"Good morning, Roberto. Sorry about the short notice," Roger said.

"I was glad to receive your call," the pilot said as he took the bags and put them inside. As Gia approached, he said, "Welcome, miss."

"Thank you." Gia took Roger's hand as he helped her inside.

Looking around, she thought: *If I'm about to die, at least I'll die in style.* The helicopter was fully loaded. If it wasn't for the fact it was about to be flying high above the city, she would've thought it was more like a limo. Maybe even better.

"You'll want to buckle up," Roger said.

She found her lap belt, did as he suggested, then immediately gripped the arms of the white leather captain's chair she was in. Roger sat to the right of her, and once he was settled, he reached over and covered her hand with his. It helped, but no matter what, this was going to be tough.

She turned to look at him, and his expression wasn't one that was relaxed either. If she wasn't in such a state herself, she'd ask him what was wrong. Maybe later. Right now, she held her breath as the helicopter lifted off. *God, please don't crash.* Her eyes were squeezed so tight they hurt, and she was pretty sure her nails were digging into the leather arm.

"It'll get better once we're up," Roger said softly.

She had no choice but to breathe, but her eyes weren't opening. If he asked, she could tell him she was thinking about her dad. That was true. If it wasn't for him, her ass never would be on this thing. *What I do for the ones I love.*

Gia felt guilty. She had promised her parents to make an effort to come home more often, but didn't. It had nothing to do with avoiding them. It was just too hard to flip the switch from Boston: always-in-a-rush mode, to Maplesville: get-to-it-when-we-can mode. And when she did go and stay with them, her parents did what all parents do: nag her about marriage and children, like that was the only option for a woman. They thought she focused too much on her career and would be an old spinster someday.

That was funny, because as long as she had Vickie around, that would never happen. All she needed to do was give Vickie the green light and she'd hook Gia up on a hundred blind dates, all local guys. But this trip wasn't a visit. And hopefully it wasn't a goodbye either. There was so much she had yet to tell her dad. A zillion things came to mind, but the only one that mattered was, *I love you.*

"Are we almost there?" she asked.

"About halfway," Roger replied.

She opened her eyes and noticed his were closed. Maybe he was tired. They didn't sleep much last night. But that wouldn't explain the tense jaw. Was he upset their getaway was cut short? He hadn't appeared to be earlier, but something was definitely off.

Gia was about to ask when it flooded back to her. *Oh my God.* Roger was doing this for her. The stiffness within him made perfect sense. How could she have forgotten? His parents died in a helicopter crash.

He'd been covering her hand with his so far. She slipped hers out and covered his. He opened his eyes and turned to her. "Not scared any longer?"

It was odd, but in that very moment, she wasn't. "No. I have you here, remember?"

He smiled down at her. "That you do." Then he said, "Did you want to call and check on your father?"

She had her cell phone in her pocket and was tempted to. But she was also afraid of what she might learn. "I'm not sure."

"Is there anyone with your mother?"

That was a good question. "My brother might be there. Normally he's at work, but I'm sure Mom called him."

"That's good. Maybe you can call him and get a status update."

Roger didn't understand her family dynamics. She couldn't remember the last time they called each other. Her brother was twelve years older than she was. There was no doubt in Gia's mind that she was a surprise late-in-life baby. Her parents were forty when she was born. By the time she was interested in doing things, her brother was thinking about moving out and starting a family of his own. Of course, he was married and divorced a few years later.

"I think I'll wait till I'm there."

"It won't be long now."

"Good." She was ready to get off this thing and have her

feet planted on the ground. "I'll see if Vickie can meet us and give us a ride to the hospital."

"I've made arrangements for a car to meet us."

She smiled up at him. "You've thought of everything." She wanted to ask him why. He could've easily stayed in New York, or let her leave and make her way back home on her own. She knew he had plenty of things he needed to take care of. Mostly things she wasn't supposed to either know or talk about. Roger seemed to be surrounded by a world of secrets and mystery. And all she knew was what they'd learned in regards to the photo yesterday. But the look in his eyes said he meant it; he wasn't leaving her. It felt nice. *But remember, this is all a dream. Eventually, we have to face reality and this will . . . end.* Gia was glad this wasn't the day. She needed Roger, even though she wasn't willing to admit it to him. If she did, it'd probably send him running in the opposite direction.

"I know you had more important things on your mind."

That's for damn sure. "I'm really sorry about having to cut the trip short."

"Nothing there appealed to me," he said, then added, "besides you."

There was no hint that he was teasing her as he spoke. "At least we had last night."

With a wink he added, "And this morning."

"Yes, that too." How quickly everything had gone from amazing and into panic mode. "I'm glad I heard the phone."

"Me too. This is where you belong."

"You've been so sweet to me, Roger. I can't even imagine how much this flight cost, never mind the hotel stay."

"Don't worry about it," Roger said.

But she did. Gia didn't want to feel as though she owed him anything. It was one thing to have a romantic night together, one where he paid for dinner. But what was she bringing into this? She didn't want to feel as though he was out of her league, but how else could she feel?

"Roger, let me at least pay for the flight." God only knew how much that would be or where she'd come up with the money, but somehow, she would.

"It didn't cost anything," Roger replied.

"Free? I have a hard time believing that."

"It's true."

She gave him a questioning look. "Did you win it?"

"No. But I own it."

Gia was shocked. He had to be kidding, right? This was a luxurious helicopter, and even a cheap one wasn't cheap. "This is yours?"

"Yes. I don't like to fly, but my job requires me to do things I'd rather not at times."

That explained how he was able to request one so quickly. If she hadn't been so focused on packing, she would've asked more questions.

"Neither of us enjoy flying, but here we are."

"And there is Providence," Roger said as he pointed out the state house.

"Hope you don't mind if I don't lean over to look."

He chuckled. "I understand perfectly." Squeezing her hand gently, he added, "I'm really proud of you."

"What for?"

"It takes courage to do something that terrifies you. If you hadn't told me about your fear before, I never would've known how hard this was for you."

She wrinkled her nose. "I think your leather seat might be a giveaway. I hope there's no damage."

"I'm sure there isn't. Well, at least not yet. We're about to start our decent."

Immediately, she tensed all over again. "No other options?"

He laughed. "Yes, but I figured jumping out of the helicopter would be a little worse."

Nodding, she closed her eyes and said, "Let me know when we're there."

She felt a kiss on the top of her head and heard him whisper, "I've got you."

Before she knew it, not only were they on the ground, but the limo had dropped them off at the emergency room entrance. She rushed in and gave the receptionist her father's name then went to sit with Roger.

"They said I have to wait. There are too many people in the room already."

"Would you like me to go and talk to them?"

She shook her head. "As long as he's not alone, that's all that matters."

"No, it's not. I'll be right back."

She watched as Roger walked up to the same receptionist she'd spoken to. The woman waved her hand, calling her over. Gia got up and went to stand by Roger.

"I called, and you can go in for a few minutes. But they are about to take him down for testing, so you can't stay long."

Gia nodded as the automatic doors opened to let her inside. She turned to Roger and said, "Thank you so much."

He nodded and replied, "I'll be right here, waiting for you."

As she followed the nurse through the doors she thought: *Share some of that strength. I think I'm going to need it.*

Roger hated sitting there. It reminded him of when his partner had been fighting for his life, and there wasn't a damn thing Roger could do to help. He'd sat in a waiting room much like this one. When the doctor came out and told him there was nothing they could do, Roger knew, he was done with the DEA.

It'd been a tough decision to leave it. Larry had tried everything to keep him. He'd been with them for ten years. Agents before had lost their lives. Yet for Roger, that moment had been his breaking point. For him, there was no going back. He knew if he did, he'd be a bigger liability than an asset.

Thankfully Caydan was looking for help. It might not have been in the same line of work, but it was enough to keep his mind distracted. But in the hospital, there was no escaping the flashbacks, threatening to return, and he needed to get out of there. He needed . . . air.

Stepping outside, he immediately felt better. He knew he couldn't be outside for long. He wanted to be there when Gia returned, as promised. A guy leaned against the wall, smoking a cigarette.

"I hate being here," the guy said.

"Won't argue about that."

"Guess it's better waiting than being the patient. But if you asked my mother, she might tell you something different." He pulled out a pack and asked, "You want one?"

Roger shook his head. "I don't smoke."

The guy took a long drag, dropped it to the ground, crushed it out, and went back inside. Roger was glad the guy wasn't in the mood for chatting. The only thing on his mind right now was Gia. It had taken some persuasion to get them to allow Gia in. No way in hell would they have allowed in a non-family member.

He was about to go back inside when his phone rang. One

look and he knew he didn't want to take the call. What he had to say really should be said in person. But if he blew Brice off, he would just call back.

"Not a good time, Brice. Can I call you back?"

"Are you still in New York?" Brice asked.

"No. Why?"

"Is Gia with you?"

"That's none of your business," Roger said firmly.

"If you're working on—"

"I'm not." He didn't need or want Brice reminding him to keep his mouth shut. He needed Brice to back the fuck off and let him do his job. Hendersons were tough and also a little paranoid, for good reason. But Roger wasn't one of the people they had to worry about. *At least not any more.*

"Have you found anything else?"

"Yes, and I'll be back in Boston tomorrow. We can talk then."

"My office first thing."

Roger didn't answer to Brice. He looked through the glass doorway and saw Gia entering the waiting area again. He didn't have time for Brice's bullshit. "I'll call you and let you know when." He ended the call and put his phone in his back pocket as he went back inside. The guy who'd been smoking outside was with her.

He could see the stress on her face. He wanted to ask how her father was, but he wasn't sure who the other guy was.

"Roger, this is my brother Gary, Gary this is my . . . friend, Roger."

"I didn't know you were with Gia." Gary leaned over. "Do me a favor, don't mention to my mother I was smoking out there. She'll flip."

"You were what?" Gia snapped. "Dad just suffered a massive heart attack and you're smoking?"

"Looks like I'm not the one you need to worry about," Roger said.

"Gia, don't start. Mom already laid into me. Hell, I've been smoking longer than you've been alive," Gary snarled.

"You should've quit a long time ago. Dad should've too," Gia added.

Roger wanted to defuse the situation. They could argue about it later, when things were calmer. "Gia, how's your father?"

She turned to him and said, "He had a heart attack. We won't know the damage for a few days. They've admitted him and transferred him to the ICU."

"I'm sorry," he said, putting an arm around her.

Gia rested her head on his chest. "He still wasn't conscious when I saw him."

"Why don't we get something to eat and wait? Maybe there'll be more news when we come back."

"I can't leave my mother alone."

Gary said, "A little late for that now don't you think?"

Roger clenched his fist. Brother or not, he didn't like anyone speaking to her like that. "Watch your words."

Gary looked at him and said, "I'm not saying anything that isn't true."

Before Roger could respond Gia said, "I am hungry. There's a little diner down the street. How about we get some breakfast?"

For Gia, he let it go. Taking her hand in his he said, "Breakfast sounds good."

They walked to the diner, which seemed to do Gia some good. By the time they arrived, he could see some of her tension eased. The hostess seated them by the window and brought them menus.

"Specials are on the board. Just wave someone down when you're ready to order."

The woman needed training in customer service.

"Guess they're all out of smiles," Gia said.

Roger turned to her and laughed. "I just checked the board. It's a Friday only special."

Gia smiled. "Then I'll just have eggs and toast."

Roger waved for a waitress, who, unlike the hostess, was bubbly. A bit too much for Roger. Smiling was one thing, but she was a chatterbox. He wasn't in a rush, but he knew Gia wanted to get back to the hospital quickly. "If you don't mind, we need to get back to the hospital and I'm starving."

The waitress nodded and said, "Let me know if you need anything else."

Let's start with what we ordered first. "She was . . . pleasant."

"I wonder if they gave all the happy pills to her," Gia said.

The waitress returned with coffee for him and tea for Gia. When she left, Roger asked, "How is your mother holding up?"

"She's angry. She said the doctor had told my father he needed to quit smoking. My father is a stubborn man. Obviously, he didn't listen. That's why my mother yelled at Gary earlier. When I told her she was wasting her breath on him, she got angry at me. So I guess the only one not angry is my father. And that's only because he's not conscious."

He reached over and held her hand. "Stress doesn't always bring out the best in people."

"No. It's more than that. It's my fault."

"What is?"

"The distance between us. I'm the one who left. But I was never really there."

Roger had nothing to say. He went to boarding school because his parents traveled the world, building their empire. What was a normal family? One that sat down for dinner every night? A mother who made sure her child did his homework? He knew he was loved. But Roger also knew he didn't fit in their lifestyle.

Gia continued. "I'm closest to my father. Mom said I was Daddy's little girl and could do no wrong in his eyes. And now he's lying in that bed and I'm . . . I'm . . ."

"Scared."

She nodded. Roger got up and threw money on the table. "What are you doing?"

"Let's go back to the hospital."

"But your food."

Roger took her hand and guided her up. "You need to be there when he wakes up."

She smiled at him and nodded. "Thank you for understanding."

Even though his relationship with his parents wasn't a conventional one, he still missed them every day. If he had the chance to tell them one more time that he loved them, or hear that they loved him, he'd trade the small fortune he inherited.

When they arrived at the hospital, he walked her to the ICU. "You know I can't go in."

"I know. Roger, I can't thank you enough for what you did for me today. But I think . . . I'm going to stay here with my mother and Gary."

"Good. Call me if you need *anything.*"

She nodded.

"No honey, I mean it," Roger said more firmly.

"I know you do." She got on tippy toes and placed a light

kiss on his lips. "And once he's stable, I'll be ready to help you again."

"I wasn't talking about that, and you know it. Now go, and I'll text you later to check in."

He knew if he didn't turn and walk away, she'd stand outside the ICU doors forever. As he walked down the hall, he heard the door open. Roger was proud of her for doing what was probably extremely difficult to do. But if things turned for the worse with her father, she was going to be glad she was there.

I wish I had had the chance to say goodbye to my parents.

CHAPTER 10

Roger could've easily met with Brice yesterday when he returned to Boston, but fuck it. He wasn't about to be dictated to by anyone. He also wanted to make sure he was available if Gia reached out and needed him ASAP. He was unsure if it was a good or bad sign that he hadn't heard from her since he left.

It was good news as far as her father being stable. He only wished things were going a bit more smoothly with Gia and her brother. Although they had only met briefly, Gary didn't seem to be anything like Gia. She was outgoing and happy and Gary seemed . . . *angry.*

But Roger wasn't sure if Gary was angry at her so much as with himself. From what Gia had told him, Gary's life hadn't turned out as he thought. Divorced and still in his hometown probably hadn't been his dream. Gary might not resent Gia as much as he was jealous of her. Man or woman, Gia had proven herself to be a fighter, willing to work to achieve what she wanted. The Henderson family would be lucky to have her.

As he rode the elevator to Brice's office, Roger questioned hooking her up with them. It wasn't as though she couldn't have applied and got the job on her own. Hell, they'd have been stupid to turn her down. Yet when Brice started to question what she knew, he was concerned he might confront Gia directly someday. Roger knew she would have a difficult time not speaking the truth.

That left only one thing. He needed to take the brunt of it, as he should. If Brice was going to be pissed, it shouldn't be at Gia. Hell, he really should thank her because she took the bull by the horns and ran with it. Roger really didn't do anything. Not that he couldn't have accomplished the same thing himself, but sadly, he didn't give a shit about the picture. At least he hadn't. After what Gia uncovered, that changed.

The doors opened and the receptionist greeted him. "Mr. Patrick, Mr. Henderson is expecting you. You may go right in."

He couldn't believe Brice had his staff there so damn early. It wasn't even eight in the morning. "Thank you."

"Can I bring you a coffee or anything?"

Depends on Brice's mood. I might need something stronger. Roger shook his head. He hopefully wasn't going to be there all that long. Then again, when had anything gone quickly when it came to a Henderson?

Brice was sitting behind a large mahogany desk that didn't fit him. The guy was a scientist. Shouldn't his office be high-tech? Instead it looked like something Brice's father or grandfather would've had. *Hell, maybe it is.* That would be disturbing since James was one of the evilest men Roger had the pleasure of researching. Thankfully he was dead, otherwise Roger might have helped him get there.

"I wasn't sure you were going to show," Brice said without looking up from his computer.

"What part of 'I'll be there at eight gave you that impression?" Roger asked sarcastically.

Brice ignored his response and asked, "You have information for me?"

"I do. I'm just not sure this is what you were looking for." Roger pulled out a report that detailed the link between Audrey Henderson and the Lawson family. He quietly watched Brice as he read through several pages.

When he finally looked up he asked, "This is accurate?"

"It appears so."

"It's not what I expected. But then again, why would I? My grandmother was a fucked-up individual who passed that down to my father."

"Sounds like your great-grandparents weren't that great after all."

"Maybe if my grandmother had gotten some help, things might not have turned out the way they did," Brice stated.

Roger wasn't so ignorant to think people back then understood mental illness, but going to such lengths to shun her from the family was a bit drastic.

"I'm not a big believer in fate, but if they hadn't, you wouldn't exist. Neither would any of your siblings."

"With a family legacy like this, can you really say that would be a bad thing? This practically says my grandmother was capable of murder."

Roger didn't want to defend the Henderson name. But since getting to know them better, it was obvious they weren't like their father. Did that mean they weren't capable of doing some really fucked-up shit? No. They still were a family not to cross. Of course, Roger wasn't easily intimidated by that.

"It was a different time. Something must have transpired in her life that no one knew. And really, the only one who might, would've been her brother, Charles. He's dead too. In my opinion, that is where you want all this to lie. What would revealing it now do? Unless you're thinking about having a big family reunion and explaining how you're related."

Brice shook his head. "I know the Lawsons are our long-lost cousins. Let's keep them that way." He opened his desk and slid in the papers, including the photo and shut it. "Our paths haven't crossed so far. I don't see why they should start now."

"Agreed."

Brice pulled out his checkbook and started filling it out.

"I don't need or want your money," Roger said firmly. He also hadn't earned it.

Brice looked up and eyed him before saying, "There's something else you want."

"Exactly."

Closing his checkbook Brice asked, "What now?"

"Loyalty."

"Why do I have a feeling we are not talking about you."

Roger had underestimated Brice. "These results were not obtained by me alone."

"Gia?" Brice asked. Roger nodded. "What the fuck part of *no one* didn't you understand? It would be one thing if it was someone who didn't know us. But you're asking me to hire her when she knows this shit about my grandmother?"

"I am." What could Brice do? Tell Gia she didn't have a job? That didn't seem like a wise thing to do.

"Give me one reason why I should?"

Brice was probably expecting him to threaten or black-mail him. Both were viable options. Neither would secure what was best for Gia. Roger did what he knew was best.

"Simple. You put all the reasons why in your drawer. Not because she knows, but because she's that damn good. Every single thing you just read was information she uncovered. I verified it, but she didn't miss the mark on one single thing."

"This skill wasn't on her résumé."

"No. I'm not sure she's aware of it. But in the right position, she'll figure it out."

Brice leaned back and said, "It sounds like she would fit better in your line of work than mine."

Maybe if I hadn't slept with her. "That's not possible."

He nodded. "I understand how difficult it is when someone you care about works so closely to you. Lena actually worked for me for a short time."

"That seemed to work out. You two are married with a growing family."

Brice laughed. "Only because I fired her. If not, I never would've gotten anything done."

Roger could see that as being a problem. "I'm sure she was thrilled not to have to see your face twenty-four/seven."

"Won't argue with you there. I'm one lucky man. So where is this going with Gia?"

Roger had no idea. And he wasn't about to discuss it with Brice. At least not in detail. "She's nice."

"Nice?" Brice cocked a brow. "I'm wondering how she'd describe you. Maybe I should ask Lena."

"How would she know?"

"Oh, women seem to know shit we don't. It took me a while to figure this out, but we're usually the last to know."

"Know what?" Roger asked.

"Everything. Meaning, you're here, speaking on her behalf. If you think this won't blow up in your face one day, you're mistaken. If you're smart, which I doubt, you'll come clean with everything."

That wasn't going to happen. "There's no reason she needs to know why she got the job." Gia knew he opened the door, but let her believe they hired her on her own merit. That was partially true.

"There's one."

"What is that?" Roger asked.

"If you see yourself having a future with her."

That was the problem. Roger couldn't see that. Not because she wasn't good enough, but because he wasn't. She had shared more about herself than he had. That's who he was. He opened up more with Gia than he ever had, but it wasn't enough. Not to sustain a relationship. Hell, things with Gia had already gotten out of control, moved too fast. Which was unlike him. He'd mastered holding in feelings for a long time. There was no denying it; he cared deeply for her. And that's why he knew they couldn't be together. She deserved better than him. Someone who could give her a close loving family, and all he had was himself. *And I'm not all that great of a catch to start.*

"I'll keep that in mind. I see it differently."

"Somehow I thought you would. You're so thickheaded, I wouldn't have been surprised if you came back telling me that you're family."

Roger snorted. "Hell no. I'm not that fucked up."

"Pretty damn close." Brice leaned back in his chair. "I'll talk to my brothers and see what we can find for Gia. My gut says my brother-in-law would be the best option."

Bennett Stone definitely was in a field that would allow Gia to grow, however it also might throw her into the line of fire. "In a desk job, right?"

Brice shook his head. "Okay, so Bennett is out. We'll find something."

"Good."

"My wife told me to invite you both for dinner tonight."

"How did she know you were going to see me today?" Roger asked.

"Like I said, they know everything."

Roger said, "I'm not sure Gia can make it. Her father is ill, and she went home to be with him."

"Is it serious?" Brice asked.

"Yes. I'm going to see her when I leave here."

"Let me know if you need anything. And don't forget, we have a lot of connections in the medical field."

"Thanks." It wasn't his place to make any decisions or give any advice. All he could do was to be there and support Gia the best he could. "Please tell Lena, thank you for the invitation."

"I will. Should I assume this means you'll be hanging around Boston a bit longer?"

Roger shook his head. "I have a beach house waiting for me. But you know how to find me if you need me." *Hopefully you won't.*

He left and headed to his car. Roger didn't want to worry, but he did. Gia hadn't reached out, and his gut said that wasn't a good thing. Before he pulled away he sent her a quick text.

GOOD MORNING. HOW ARE THINGS WITH YOUR FATHER?

He waited but there was no immediate response. His stomach sank, and he wanted to dial her number. But he'd told her he'd be there if she needed him. Maybe she didn't need him. That was good. She was a strong, independent woman. It was okay if she didn't need him.

So why was not being with her bothering him so damn much? This was what he wanted. He wasn't staying in Boston. Yet leaving without saying goodbye sure as hell wasn't what he wanted either.

What the hell? Roger threw the car in drive and headed toward Rhode Island. He had no idea what he would encounter, or what he was going to say, but he wanted . . . no needed, to see her. It sickened him to think he was being as . . . controlling as the Hendersons, but hell, the rule book went out the window the moment he met her. He'd lost track of how many he'd already broken. *Just one I can't afford to: Don't break her heart.*

Gia couldn't keep her eyes open a moment longer. Lying across the hard plastic seats in the ICU waiting room was far from ideal. But Gary left to go to work, and her mother was sleeping in the chair beside her father. Even though her mother said she could go home and get some rest, Gia wasn't ready to head back to Boston.

The only thing she wished she had right now was a power cord for her cell phone. It had died late last night after chatting with Roger. She had told him they'd talk today, but apparently the universe had other plans. It was funny, she remembered a lot of things, but couldn't recall Vickie's or Roger's phone numbers. It was sad how she relied on technology, and the two people she really wanted to talk to right now, were out of her reach.

She closed her eyes. *Where are my shooting stars when I need them?* There was so much for her to wish for right now; the stars could light up the sky and she'd have a wish for each of them.

It wasn't easy to sleep with the loud intercom paging doctors directly overhead. But somehow, exhaustion kicked in and sleep came. It was far from peaceful as she was tortured with thoughts of Roger. Not the sweet tender moments they had shared just two day ago, but one of heartbreak. He walked away. His back was to her. No matter how loud she called, he didn't turn around.

The tears burned as they streamed down her cheeks. How could he do this? Didn't he know how much she needed him? She called out again, and he increased his pace, as though he couldn't put enough distance between them.

She knew that was coming. His life wasn't in Boston. How could she have expected him to stay? Just like the people wanted her to stay in Maplesville. You can't be where your heart wasn't. But he took a piece of her heart with him.

It wasn't fair. When she was with him she felt . . . the most alive she ever had. They might have just crossed paths, yet something about them together felt so . . . right. Gia was a fighter and wasn't letting him go this easily.

She got up and started to chase after him. Yet her feet wouldn't move. She was stuck to the ground. When she looked down, the sandy beach was replaced with concrete and her feet were covered, holding her in place. As she looked around, tall building rose from below and eventually blocked her view. The answer was there. They had chosen different lives, and those differences would keep them apart.

She sobbed, missing him with all she was, then she heard someone calling her. *Gia. Gia. Wake up.* Her eyes flew open; thankful it was only a dream. He was there. Roger was in front of her.

But as her foggy brain cleared, it wasn't him. Gary had returned. She couldn't lie to herself; she was disappointed it wasn't Roger, yet shocked Gary came back. "I thought you could use some coffee."

Gia sat up, taking the paper cup from him. She appreciated the thought, but it only showed once again how little they knew about each other. She never drank coffee. Actually she hated the taste. But she didn't want to return the tension that was between them yesterday. So she took a sip and smiled.

"Thank you. I thought you were going to be at work all day."

"I was, but I couldn't focus. My boss sent me home."

She could relate. Gia slid over, making space for him to sit. "Have you talked to Mom yet?"

"No. I wanted to check on you first. You look tired. Why don't you go home and get some sleep?"

"Boston is not next door."

Gary said, "I meant Maplesville. You know your room is still there. Hell, so is mine. Nothing in that house is ever going to change."

"From what the doctor said, they aren't going to have a choice. The place needs too much work, and there are too many stairs. Mom and Dad are in their seventies. They shouldn't be living alone." She worried about them, even though she didn't want to give up her independent life and move home. She had worked so hard to get where she was, only to walk away from it all now.

"Mom isn't going to like it, but I think you and I should sit down and have a serious talk with her."

"Gary, she's not going to listen to me." They had never seen eye to eye on small things. Talking about giving up the family home and relocating wasn't going to go well.

"There's things you don't know."

That didn't surprise her. For years she'd been out of the loop. Both intentional and because of distance. "Would you like to fill me in?"

He nodded. "This wasn't Dad's first heart attack."

Her eyes widened in shock. There was no way. Someone would've told her. "You're not serious." He nodded. "Why am I just hearing about that now?"

Gary reached out and put a hand on her shoulder. "Because even though none of us ever told you, we're all very proud of what you've accomplished. You said you were going to make it, and you did. Hell, if I had half of your perseverance, I might have been able to make my marriage work."

It seemed unreal. Was the wedge there all this time because she put it there? That didn't make sense, yet there was no reason for Gary to lie about such a thing. What they had thought or done in the past didn't matter. This was about her parents. She knew this day would come, but somehow, it felt like it was too soon.

"Gary, tell me what you want me to say to Mom and I will."

He laughed. "You're the brains of the bunch. One thing I know about you: when you want something, you don't stop until you get it."

For years she wanted to hear these words, but she never wanted to use them on her mother. "She's going to be . . . resistant."

"That's putting it lightly."

Gia ran several options through her mind, but none seemed to end well. Most would become a shouting match, which definitely wouldn't accomplish anything. When she was about to give up and tell Gary he needed to be the one, she noticed Roger standing in the doorway.

"How long have you been standing there?" From the look on his face, he hadn't just arrived.

"Long enough. Your brother is right; you can do this."

All their confidence in her abilities was way overstated. "Roger, she is going to want me to be there to help. How can I make that promise when my job is in Boston?"

"Parents don't want you to give up your life. They want to know you're there if they need you."

"Isn't that the same thing? I can't commit to working for the Hendersons, knowing I might need to drop everything and rush back here."

"True, but you can help them without physically being here. You're a very resourceful woman. Use that now."

He was right. Gia was thinking with her emotions instead of her head. If this was a business she needed to put into compliance, what would be her first course of action? *Get the doctors all on the same page and in our corner.*

"Guess I have my work cut out for me," Gia said.

Gary added, "*We* do. You're not in this alone."

She leaned over and hugged him. Gia couldn't remember the last time they talked like this, never mind hugged. Just then their mother entered the room.

"I never thought I'd see this day," she said, her eyes filled with tears.

Gia and Gary both got up and rushed over to her. "Is it Dad?"

She shook her head. "Your father's fine."

"Then what's the matter?" Gia asked.

"Nothing. For the first time in a long time, everything is right." She wrapped her arms around them both. "I only wish your father could've seen this."

Gia met Gary's eyes and they both knew, this wouldn't be the last time. It was going to take effort on both of their parts, but family was worth it. *To be there when needed.*

Out of the corner of her eye, she saw Roger turn and walk away. *No. Don't go.* Leaving and rushing after him might be what she wanted to do, but not what was the best to do. It felt like her dream, but the obstacle wasn't Boston, it wasn't a job either. It was something greater than either of those things. *It's family.*

Tightening her grip on her mother, they all stood there, holding each other. Then her mother said, "Your father is awake and wants to see you both."

Gia's eyes watered, and she fought back the tears as all three of them walked into the ICU. She didn't know what tomorrow was going to bring for her parents, but it no longer scared her, because they were going to face it together.

The only thing missing is Roger. But he hadn't left her. He showed up when she needed him, and deep inside she knew he would again. *He's been doing that since the day we met.*

CHAPTER 11

She almost forgot about her interview. Gia almost called Brittney to cancel, but both her mom and Gary told her, more like insisted, to go. It was funny how they tried to prepare her with off-the-cuff questions. Not saying that it had been a while since either of them had been interviewed, but the questions they asked were illegal.

Yet as she sat with Brittney, who was totally professional, she knew she didn't need to worry about it.

"Would there be any issue with you starting next week?" Brittney asked.

Gia hadn't expected the job offer to come immediately, and wished she had time to discuss it with her family, but wishing was worthless. It was decision time. *Family or future?* So much to weigh on, and she didn't have time to stall. Any delay in response might play negatively on her. Then she remembered Roger. He said to use her skills to obtain what she wanted. Surely he wasn't talking just about her family. It was in her life in general.

Holding her head up high, and internally crossing her

fingers, Gia stated, "If it wouldn't be an inconvenience, I'd prefer to make it the following week."

Brittney didn't even blink an eye and said, "That works as well. In the meantime, I'll email you what information you might need to know prior to your first day. Are there any questions you have for me?"

Gia shook her head. "Not at this time. Thank you again for meeting with me so early."

"It actually worked out. The Hendersons are all in town and called a meeting. If we made it any later, I would've been forced to reschedule. I'll walk you out."

"Thank you." She gathered things and followed Brittney to the elevator. As the doors opened, a tall well-dressed man was getting out.

"Brittney, I was just coming to see you. My wife hoped you could meet with her regarding HR policies later today. Would you be available?"

"Of course. Please let Allyson know we can meet whenever is most convenient for her. By the way, let me introduce our latest employee to you. This is Gia Gravel. Gia, this is Caydan Pintino. One of your new bosses."

Roger had spoke about a friend named Caydan, but he was a Henderson. Once again, she knew there was a story behind it all. If Roger was still in Boston, she'd ask. *What the heck?* He was gone, and she was very capable of finding things out on her own. *Managed okay before Roger, I can after him too.* "It's a pleasure to meet you. I heard your name before. Would you know a Roger Patrick?"

Caydan cocked a brow. He looked her over, and she wondered if asking had been wise. "What are you doing for dinner?"

She wasn't anticipating that response. "I . . . I don't have any plans." That wasn't entirely true. Gia thought she'd be going to Maplesville and updating them on the interview.

"Could you join my wife and me for dinner?"

Like saying no was really an option. Brittney just said he was her boss. But why he was inviting her was a mystery.

"Yes, I can. Was there something you'd like to discuss with me?"

"No. Why?"

"I wanted to be prepared if needed." Gia had been out with Lena for lunch, hopefully Allyson would be as warm and friendly. It was hard to gauge, since Caydan seemed . . . standoffish. "Would you like me to meet you someplace?"

Caydan pulled out his phone and typed something before answering her. "How about six and here?"

"Excellent. I'll see you then." She turned back to Brittney, "Thank you again, and I'll see you in two weeks."

When her feet finally hit the sidewalk, a limo pulled up. Her heart skipped a beat, hoping it was Roger. Although they texted daily, it wasn't the same as seeing him. He was being so damn thoughtful, trying to give her time and space to do what she needed to. What he didn't seem to understand was how much she needed him. They had become close in such a short time, but that didn't mean she didn't feel his absence.

But when the driver walked around and opened the door she knew it wasn't Roger. He never let anyone hold a door for him. To her surprise, it was Lena. She rushed right over and gave her a hand getting out.

"Thank you Gia," Lena said as she stabled herself. "Can you believe they're having a meeting and forgot to ask me?"

Gia chuckled. "I'm sure it was an oversight."

Lena rubbed her belly. "I'm going to guess they didn't want me delivering on the conference room table. I'm okay with natural childbirth, but that would be more natural than I want."

"Are you going in anyway?" Gia asked then realized it was none of her business.

Lena shook her head. "Actually I was here hoping I'd catch you before you left."

"Me?"

"Yes. I wanted to know how your father was doing."

Had Roger told her? "Better. They had to insert stents in a few arteries, but thankfully he didn't require open heart surgery. Tomorrow we take him home."

"Do you need any help? Or your mother?"

Gia really didn't know how they were going to manage everything. The biggest issue right now was how they were going to finically make ends meet. That wasn't something she was going to share with anyone, not even Roger.

"My brother, Gary, lives close by. But thank you." She really did appreciate Lena's offer. She knew it wasn't said just to be nice. Lena was genuinely a nice person. "So you're due—"

"Any day. Hopefully today. That's why I'm here. Hoping we can go for a walk." Lena lowered her voice even though there wasn't anyone in earshot. "Don't tell anyone, but I had a few contractions early this morning."

"You're in labor?" Gia asked, trying not to show her panic.

"Early stages I guess. But walking helps speed things along."

And that's a good thing? "Maybe you should call your doctor, or go to the hospital or—"

"Just take a walk and get ice cream."

"Not craving Thai?" Gia teased.

Lena made a face. "Goodness no. I think I've eaten ice cream for dinner for the past three days."

"I know my stomach will be happier if we stop. So where do you want to go? Boston Commons?"

"Actually I'm thinking the wharf. Nice breeze and we can watch the boats come and go. And they have a place that lets you make your own ice cream."

"And how far is it to the hospital from there?" Gia asked.

Lena shrugged. "I'm not worried about it."

That makes one of us. Gia had a feeling if she declined the offer, Lena would go on her own. Even though the limo driver would be close by, it wasn't the same thing. "I could go for some rocky road ice cream."

"Yum. Anything chocolate, or nuts or . . . heck, let's be real, I'll eat just about anything right now."

One the way to the wharf, Gia talked about the interview and how impressed she was with Brittney.

"She definitely knows her stuff. You should've heard the questions my mother asked me, thinking it would prepare me better."

"What kinds of questions," Lena asked.

"The illegal ones. Are you married? Are you thinking about getting married? Any children in your future? Any health issues?"

Lena laughed. "Your mother asked you those?" Gia nodded. "I don't think she was talking about the interview. I know how my mother used such tactics to get me to settle down. I was afraid to bring Brice around. Once she got her claws in him, it was all over." Patting her stomach, she added, "And the rest is history."

"Oh, I have a feeling your story is still in the making."

"You might be right." Lena moaned.

"Are you okay?" Gia asked. She saw Lena's expression change.

"I think you were right."

That's not what she wanted to hear. "Do you want to go to the hospital?"

She shook her head. "I want to stop at Henderson Towers. If I have to drag Brice out of that meeting kicking and screaming, he's coming with me."

"Maybe you should call ahead. Have him meet the limo when you pull up." Gia never had a baby, but from Lena's breathing, things were moving along faster than Lena may have hoped.

"Oh, boy."

Oh boy? "What?" She pulled out her cell phone not knowing what the heck to do. So she did the only thing she could think of and sent Roger a text.

WITH LENA. SHE'S IN LABOR. WHAT DO I DO?

Instead of texting her back Roger called. "Where are you?"

Not wanting Lena to know she was panicking, she tried to play it cool. "Hi Roger. I'm out with Lena. We're by the wharf and heading back to Henderson Towers."

"But she's in labor, right?" he asked.

"That's right. Not sure what you'd like me to do about that," Gia said while watching Lena.

"I'm updating Brice. You get her to a hospital."

"Tried that."

"Damn it. I'll call you right back." Roger ended the call.

"What . . . what . . . did . . . he want?" Lena asked between breaths.

"Checking how my day is going."

"Did you . . . tell him . . . uneventful?" Lena teased.

163

"Really? You can joke when you're about to deliver a baby in the back of a limo?" Gia hoped that wasn't the case.

"Just think how it will look on your résumé."

Just then Gia's phone rang as well as Lena's. There was no question by the barking she heard on Lena's that it was Brice. He was stressing he was on the way to the hospital and she better be too.

"I'll meet you there," Roger said.

"You're in Boston?" Gia asked.

"Yes," Roger replied.

Lena said, "Change of plans. We're going to the hospital."

Thank God. "Roger, if you're free, I can use a ride."

"I'm on my way," Roger said and ended the call.

I just hope we make it. The limo driver also must've been given instructions as he was beeping his horn and weaving through traffic. Boston was always busy, and today was no exception. Lena had a few more contractions, heavy if the moans were any indication. Nothing was sweeter than the limo pulling in front of the hospital and Brice waiting with a wheelchair.

The limo might not have even been put in park when Brice opened the door and asked, "How far along are the contractions?"

Lena wasn't in any position to answer, as another one had come. Gia took her best guess. "Less than two minutes. We didn't even make it through two lights on the last one."

Brice leaned over and scooped Lena up in to his arms then into the chair. "Okay, let's go have this baby."

Gia stood on the sidewalk as Brice pushed the wheelchair into the building. The driver approached her and asked, "Miss, is there someplace I can take you?"

She looked around and didn't see Roger. It was a shame to make him leave whatever he was doing when she easily could utilize the vehicle that was already at her disposal. Yet this wasn't about convenience. Gia was tired of talking through technology. She wanted to see his face. *Maybe get a hug, because God knows I need one.*

"Thank you but a . . . friend is meeting me here."

The limo driver nodded and drove away. As she waited, she realized her feet were killing her. She'd been dressed for an interview, not a walk on the wharf or standing in front of a hospital. Although tempted to go inside, she didn't want Roger to have to go looking for her. She'd give him a few more minutes, then call and check his status.

What Gia wasn't prepared for was a taxi pulling up next to her and Roger getting out. "Sorry it took me so long."

"What happened to your car?"

"I didn't have it with me." Roger said as he let her slip into the taxi then joined her.

"Roger, I didn't want to pull you away from work."

"Are you kidding me? That text message pretty much changed all the plans for the day."

"I'm sorry."

"Don't be. I have no idea why they wanted me there anyway. I'm not a Henderson."

"You were at Henderson Towers?" She hadn't seen him, then again, she'd been trying to focus on what was important, getting the job.

"I was. And tonight I was supposed to have dinner with Caydan and Allyson." Pulling her hand to his lips he added, "But I'd much rather have dinner with you." Gia chuckled. Roger asked, "Was that funny?"

"Yes, because *I'm* having dinner with Caydan and Allyson tonight."

Roger laughed. "So much for having you all to myself."

There's always later. "I'm sure we can sneak out before dessert."

"That's my girl."

Am I? She wished that was the case. Maybe then she'd tell him that she was having strong feelings for him and wished they could explore what had started to bloom. But tomorrow she'll go back to Maplesville to settle things for her parents. And Roger will go back to whatever it was he did.

Don't overthink it. Tomorrow comes fast enough. Just enjoy the moment. You don't get many of them.

Roger never should've mentioned dinner. He easily could've blown off his friends. But he didn't believe Gia would've followed suit. That was the problem with rule followers. Little white lies didn't work for them. He had to admit, that could be an issue. He knew that look on Caydan's face. Caydan had a reason for asking them both to dinner. Roger wasn't even listening to Gia tell the story of how they had met.

"That is so romantic," Allyson said.

"I'm not sure romantic would be the term I'd use, but it was memorable," Gia responded.

Roger was trying to ignore the ladies endless chatter. But it beat the hell out of whatever was on Caydan's mind. It was a conversation they'd have later. Alone. Or at least he hoped so.

"Why do you think my brother called a family meeting?" Caydan asked.

"I'm not privy to what your brother does," Roger replied.

Caydan turned to Gia and asked, "You're new with the company. Do you know?"

Roger was about to snap and tell Caydan to keep her out

of it, but even though Gia's eyes widened, she calmly said, "I'm so new that I start in two weeks. When we met earlier, I was leaving my interview."

Good girl. She didn't lie, only stated facts that didn't include anything of importance. Was that intentional? Because if so, that was another skill he didn't realize she had. *One she's going to need around the Hendersons.*

Roger watched as Caydan continued to stare at Gia. He knew this wasn't good. Caydan was fixated on her for some reason. Did he really suspect she knew something? That would be crazy, if it was true.

Fuck. This could all blow up. Brice would be pissed. Yet did he really think this kind of stuff would stay buried? The only way that would've happened would have been if he ripped that photo up the moment he'd seen it. Once Brice wanted to know more, it was inevitable others would also learn the truth. The only difference, Caydan was still building the bond with his family. Having Brice hide shit wasn't the way to keep the brotherly trust. *And covering for Brice isn't a way for me to hold a friendship either.*

This wasn't a situation he wanted to be in. Just a little over a year ago Roger was digging up dirt for Caydan to take the Hendersons down. Now Roger was out to protect them. Even Brice. He never thought he'd need to worry about Gia in this crazy mix. That's because he never imagined caring for her the way he did, never mind bringing her into this circle. The Hendersons, including Caydan, were all capable of taking care of themselves. Gia, even though he told her how strong she was, still had a vulnerable side to her. And that he'd protect at all cost.

"All I know is there's something Brice isn't telling us," Caydan said, looking at Gia.

"She said she doesn't know anything," Roger said in a flat

tone. If Caydan pushed the subject, that tone was going to change. Before Caydan tried again, Allyson interjected.

"Maybe it's the stress of the baby coming that was getting to him?"

Roger nodded. "He freaked out when I told him Lena was in labor."

"I'm so happy you did. Nothing I said was going to get Lena to go to the hospital. I thought for sure I'd be delivering a baby. Which, by the way, is not a skill I have," Gia clarified.

"Me either," Allyson added. "I really thought we'd hear something by now. It sounded like she was going to deliver right away."

Caydan chimed in, "Brice said the contractions stopped, and they are in the waiting game."

"Lena told me they missed their family Sunday brunches at her house. Maybe Brice was trying to get us all together as a family for Lena."

That's not Brice's style. By the look on Caydan's face, he knew that wasn't it either. Gia was grinning.

"I can see how she would enjoy such a thing. Of course, she's in no shape to plan it. I'm not sure how your family functions go, but in mine, men are horrible with the details. If it were up to my brother or father to plan, there'd be beer and burgers, in that order."

Allyson's eyes became bright. "Gia, you're a genius."

"I am?" Gia replied.

"Yes. We're all in Boston. Why don't we plan a family reunion?" Allyson asked.

Caydan looked at her and asked, "You're joking right?"

Allyson shook her head. "No I'm not. The last time we were all together was a year ago for our wedding. This would be great."

168

"There's no way you can take all that on yourself," Caydan said. Then added, "And I'm not helping."

"Good, because I wasn't asking you to. Like Gia said, we want this done *right*." Allyson turned to Gia and said, "We can pull this off without their help. But I know my sisters-in-law will want to get involved too."

"We?" Gia echoed.

Allyson reached across the table and said, "It was your idea, and everyone is going to want to meet you anyway. What better way than this?"

Roger looked to Gia, who seemed overwhelmed. He could easily get her out of that, but there was a part of him that wanted her to do it. Maybe so he didn't need to suffer through another Henderson event alone.

Gia looked up at him with pleading in her eyes. Instead he fed her to the wolves. "You're right, Allyson. If anyone can pull this off with such short notice, it's this woman." *Because I've underestimated her every step and always left in awe.*

Gia seemed surprised that he was encouraging her. But then she turned back to Allyson and said, "Just so you know, I'm not a party planner, but I'm organized and that can be a plus."

Allyson beamed, and Caydan shook his head then said to Roger, "I hope this means you're staying in Boston for a while. Because I'm not going to be listening to this all by myself."

Roger looked over to Gia and said, "I have no plans to go anywhere."

Gia's eyes softened as she smiled. "Then I guess we have a party to plan."

"I can't wait to tell the others. But let's not do it in Boston. I want someplace the kids can all run around and have fun too."

"I have a suggestion," Roger said. "Why don't you ladies talk about this tomorrow?"

Caydan added, "I second that motion."

The two women laughed and exchanged phone numbers. It gave Roger the perfect time to make their escape.

"Since you two will be chatting a lot, what do you say you and I head out for some alone time?"

Gia smile up at him, blushing slightly. "You did promise me dessert."

Roger's body tensed, knowing exactly what it was he wanted. She was all the sweet he needed. He turned to Caydan. "Thank you for dinner. Allyson, try and keep him out of trouble while you're in Boston."

She placed a hand on Caydan's arm. "I don't know. Trouble seems to be his middle name. Just like yours." Then she said, "I'll call you tomorrow, Gia." Giving her a wink, she added, "But not too early."

As they drove away from the restaurant, Roger asked, "Where would you like to go for dessert? I know a place with awesome strawberry shortcake, and another one known for their truffles."

"I have ice cream and hot fudge at my place," Gia said.

Interested was an understatement. He'd been aching to get her alone since he'd pulled up to the hospital. Yet taking her home, whether her apartment or his hotel, wasn't the smart thing to do. He'd never be able to keep his hands off her. Controlling his desires had never been an issue for him before. With Gia, it was different. Fuck, everything was.

He'd never taken a woman to dinner with his friends. That was too close to admitting they were a couple. Yet Roger didn't do a damn thing to dispute that assumption when it rose. Was he getting old and tired of this single life? No. He was happy the way things were. Or at least he was until two weeks ago. Those damn green eyes of hers drew him in, and everything else about her captivated him. Roger had no idea how the hell someone like her was still single. *Because there's a lot of stupid men out there. I'm probably one of them.*

"I'm tempted, trust me, very tempted, but I thought you needed to get back to Maplesville tonight?"

"I told Gary I'd be there early in the morning to relieve him before he leaves for work. Maybe we could call it an early night?"

Roger reached over and took her hand in his. "Maybe we can call it an early morning, and I drive you to your parents?"

She smiled and nodded. "I'd like that."

He wasn't sure he was ready to meet her father. He was still recovering from a heart attack, and Roger didn't want to add any undue stress on him. Gia was his baby girl, and he was going to want to make sure Roger was treating her with respect. He may have slept with her, but one thing Roger knew, he did respect and care very much about Gia. That was something he had no problem telling her father, if asked. Hopefully no one would.

No matter how much he'd like to avoid the questions, dropping her off at their doorstep would be . . . cheap. That sure as hell wasn't how he wanted their relationship portrayed. She introduced him before as a friend. Tomorrow they were about to learn just how friendly they were.

He'd stepped back and gave her space. Even now, space was still needed. But they wanted each other; that was undeniable. He didn't know if she needed him as much as he needed her. As her fingers entwined with his he had one question. *When did I start needing anyone?*

CHAPTER 12

Gia's heart was racing as they pulled up to the house. It was early because Gary needed to be at work by eight. Thankfully Roger had opted to drive his Jeep. The last thing Gia needed or wanted was Gary drooling over Roger's Maserati.

No one needed to know how wealthy Roger was. Heck, she didn't know herself. It would've been easy enough to find out if she wanted. If she could find information on people who were born more than a hundred years ago, surely Roger Patrick was less of a mystery. But she'd never googled his name. She wanted to get to know the real man, not the one the internet said he was. And really, she liked who he was. No doubt there was more to him, something in his past he either didn't want to share or wasn't ready to, but did that matter? She was looking in only one direction, the future. She just didn't know if it would include Roger or not.

"Hope that coffee is for me," Gary said as he walked outside.

Gia handed him the paper cup. "Of course. You remember Roger?"

Gary looked him over and nodded. "Yeah. Did Mom and

Dad know he was coming?" Gia shook her head. "Hell, now I want to call out of work."

Gia slapped his arm. "That's not funny. I'm a grown woman who can bring home a gentlemen friend if I want."

Gary laughed. "Phrase it any way you want. But since you've *never* brought one before, I think Roger is something special."

She heard Roger chuckle from behind her but kept her focus on Gary. "Aren't you going to be late?"

He nodded. "Don't worry about telling me how it goes. I'm sure Mom will fill me in later." Then Gary shook Roger's hand and said, "You got your hands full with this one. She's stubborn."

And deadly when riled up. Once they were alone, she said, "You don't have to come in if you don't want to." She had mixed feelings, so whatever he decided was okay with her. She was giving him an out, because Gary was nothing compared to what her mother was going to be like.

"I don't know. These blueberry scones smell awfully good. I'm not sure I can resist."

She chuckled and said, "I hope you know what you're getting yourself into."

"I have a pretty good idea," Roger replied as they walked up the front steps.

But why are you doing it? That's what has me puzzled. He'd made it clear he liked his secluded beach house. He didn't enjoy the city. And most of all, he liked being single. Roger didn't seem to have a business partner.

Sure enough her mother was sitting at the kitchen table, holding a cup of tea. She didn't look surprised to see Roger behind Gia, which meant she'd been watching them from the window.

"Good morning. So nice to see you again. Mr. Patrick, right?"

"Call me Roger, please."

"Only if you call me Claudia." Gia's father slowly entered the room. He was looking tired, but that was expected. In a few weeks he could start cardiac rehab, but he'd never be the same. But in her eyes, he'd always be her strong Dad who could move mountains if she asked him to.

Claudia added, "This is my husband, Andrew. Andrew, this is Gia's . . . friend, Roger."

Roger walked over and shook his hand. "Nice to see you're feeling better."

"Don't listen to these two. If they had their way, I'd be lying down all damn day and eating only vegetables." Andrew sat beside Claudia and said, "And that better not be something healthy in that box you're holding either."

Roger placed the box on the table and said, "It does contain fruit, blended in a sweet biscuit."

Andrew opened the box and pulled out the largest scones covered with the most sugared glaze. "Now if you'd brought me regular coffee instead of that decaffeinated crap Claudia made, I'd be in heaven."

"Dad, we're trying to make it so you don't see heaven for many more years. No caffeine, no smoking and no—"

"Sex. Got it," Andrew blurted.

Roger laughed, and Gia stood there, torn between shock and embarrassment. Clearing her throat she said, "I *was* going to say, alcohol."

Andrew turned to Roger and said, "See, they want to keep me out of heaven, by making my life hell. Why don't you pull up a seat and stay awhile. God knows I'm not going anywhere. Claudia said she misplaced the keys to my truck. I'm calling bullshit on that."

174

Roger sat next to Gia's father, and she watched as the two chatted up a storm. Gia thought for sure her parents were going to give him the third degree, but instead they talked more about Maplesville and growing up in a small, tight-knit town. Surprisingly, Roger shared stories about his childhood and the loss of his parents.

Claudia said, "It must've been very difficult growing up all alone."

"I was lucky and had good friends. But you're right, they don't replace my loss," Roger said. Then he turned to Gia and covered her hand with his. "She's lucky to have you guys."

Claudia said, "No. We're the lucky ones. Gia is so . . . different from us. We've always been laid back. Change never was something we were good at. But Gia has always embraced it. If there was a challenge, she faced it head-on. That's why, when she decided to move to Boston, we knew she'd do okay. And now with you in her life, we don't have to worry so much. She's not alone." Claudia reached over and patted his hand and added, "Andrew and I are going to celebrate our fiftieth wedding anniversary next month. It seems like just yesterday."

Andrew leaned over and kissed Claudia. "I'd do it all over again." But her father always had to end things with a joke. "But maybe I'd have sent you to cooking classes first."

Claudia slapped him playfully. "Andrew it wasn't my cooking, it was your taste buds, and you know it."

"That's true. After a year of marriage, I didn't have any left."

Claudia shook her head. "Roger, don't listen to my husband. He doesn't have a serious bone in his body."

"I sure as hell do. Mess with my pickup truck and all hell breaks loose."

175

Roger laughed. "I hear you. Don't come between a man and his truck."

"I knew I'd like you, young man," Andrew said.

Gia sat back, and for the first time in more years than she could remember, this house felt like home again. Was it the fact that her father had almost died and the petty little differences didn't matter any longer? Or had she changed enough that she found a way to appreciate not just where her future was heading, but her past as well. As she looked at her parents, she realized, her strength had come from them. *And my wit from my Dad.*

Her phone rang and Gia saw it was Allyson. She somehow had forgotten all about the family reunion. "Hello, Allyson."

"Hi. I know I said I'd let you sleep in, but I spoke to the others last night, and no one could wait. We want to start planning right away. Did you have time to meet us for lunch?"

"Lunch? Today?" Gia asked.

"If you're free," Allyson said.

Claudia nodded. "Don't you sit around here. Your father and I are dying for some quiet time. He's going to do his crosswords and I'm finishing a book."

Gia looked at Roger. "You volunteered yourself for this."

Gia covered the phone, "I think you have a problem with your short-term memory. I'm positive it was you."

Andrew laughed, "You sound just like your mother."

Claudia huffed. "Gia, you're exactly like your father, and you know it."

Gia rolled her eyes and returned to her phone call. "Lunch will be fine. Just text me the place and time."

"Perfect. My sisters-in-law can't wait to meet you." Allyson ended the call, leaving Gia wondering why they needed her if they were all pitching in. Maybe at lunch she could convince them she'd really be in the way. *Without Roger around to throw me under the bus, I might be able to weasel out of this.*

She slipped her phone into her purse and said, "I guess we better head back to Boston."

They got up, and her mother walked over and gave Roger a huge hug. "I hope we see you again soon."

"I'm sure you will," Roger replied.

Then her father said, "The door's always open, just stop on by. And feel free to bring dessert anytime you want."

"Dad, you know what the doctor said," Gia warned.

He nodded and whispered, "Don't get caught."

Gia reached for Rogers hand and said, "We better leave these two alone to discuss this." Roger grinned as he took hold of her hand.

Even before they were out the door she heard her mother yapping at her father.

"Andrew, I can't believe you are trying to get that nice man in trouble."

"Claudia, I don't think he needs my help for that. Remember, he's with *our* daughter."

When they got into his Jeep, Gia couldn't believe how good the visit had been. Was this considered to be a normal family? *Who knows. But this is what mine is like.*

Roger hated dropping Gia off, but he had a few things to take care of. Mostly, he needed to find out why the heck Brice had pulled the family together. Had he suddenly changed his mind and decided to let them in on the family's latest disgusting development? Brice might not be the most tactful person, but

177

he'd never invited everyone. Maybe his brothers, but that would be it.

Once again, he got voicemail. He wasn't leaving him a message as this wasn't critical. Brice was doing what he needed to, being there for his wife and child. That left Roger with some free time. *Might as well see what Caydan wanted me for.*

Caydan answered right away. "Figured I'd hear from you."

"You mean since your wife dragged—"

"Your girlfriend away?" Caydan joked.

"I'm sure that's not what you wanted to talk about, right?" Roger knew Caydan didn't like wasting time anymore than he did.

"No. What I really want to know is what the hell my dear brother Brice is up to? And since when are you so chummy with him?" Caydan demanded.

This conversation couldn't take place over the phone. At least it shouldn't. They'd been friends for too damn long to not clear the air. "How far are you from my hotel?"

"I'm in the lobby, on my way up."

I should've known. "Door's open."

A few minutes later his suite's door swung open, and Caydan shut it behind him. Then he walked to the bar and poured himself a bourbon. "Want one?"

"I'm good."

Once Caydan was seated, Roger did the same.

"So tell me what's going on. And none of this bullshit that there's nothing. You've never been a fan of my family, yet I've heard you've been seen with Brice a few times."

"You're right, and I'm still not a fan. I'm speaking as your friend." Although he knew the saying, blood was thicker than water, he knew that didn't always apply.

"Meaning what you tell me, stays here?" Caydan asked. Roger nodded. "Okay. Spill it."

"Brice asked me to research a photo that his . . . I mean that *your* father had hidden away." Roger was never going to get used to calling James Henderson, Caydan's father. By the look of Caydan's clenched jaw, neither was Caydan.

"What did you find?"

"Actually, more than I thought I would. The Hendersons have cousins out there."

"That's all? I figured there was a ninth child out there."

Roger laughed. "I'm not saying there isn't, but that has yet to be determined."

"So what is the big deal? Cousins. Who cares?"

Roger let out a long exhale. "Has anything ever been that fucking cut and dry with your family?" Caydan shook his head. "All I can say is count your blessings you weren't raised by that asshole. And you never met your grandmother either. If so we probably wouldn't be friends now."

"I know my grandmother was abusive to James. But I can tell there is more."

Roger spent the next hour telling him everything Gia had uncovered. It was probably harder updating Caydan than it had been telling Brice. Caydan had been through enough, and for once, he'd like to deliver him some good news about his family history. It was one fucked-up family tree no one wanted to be on.

Caydan sat there for a minute afterward as though still trying to process it all. "And Brice doesn't want us to know, why?"

"As far as I could tell, the Lawson family has no clue as to what a fucking asshole their great-grandfather was. This knowledge getting out would have a ripple effect. It's bad enough the Hendersons had to suffer for his actions. What good would it be having the Lawsons do so as well?"

"Roger, I love my family, but damn it, sometimes I wish I never knew. The hate I had carried inside, at times, is less painful than the love. Not sure that makes much sense."

Since he was the one who been there every step of the way, Roger got it. "Ignorance is bliss."

"Exactly. Thanks for telling me, but I agree with Brice. We tell no one."

"And if it gets out?" Roger asked.

"Then we do what Henderson blood seems to do best."

Roger cocked a brow. "What is that?"

Caydan downed his drink and said, "We try to make amends for what our ancestors fucked up."

From where Roger sat, it seemed like they were going to spend a lifetime doing so. But he had to give them credit. At least they were trying.

"I'm glad that's out of the way," Roger said.

"Me too. So now we can talk about Gia. Why the hell do I need to hear it from Allyson that you are serious about her?"

"Damn it. Brice was right."

Caydan asked, "About what?"

"They are always a step ahead of us." Roger laughed. "And I just realized, I'm in fucking trouble."

"How so?"

"Gia is not just with Allyson. She's meeting up with the Henderson clan of women."

Caydan burst out laughing. "You might as well give up and put a ring on her finger now."

Roger shook his head. "Don't you start on my ass too. Besides, it's too fast. There's so much we don't know about each other. And I'm actually looking forward to learning more, at a normal pace. You know, dating. Not sure if you ever heard of it."

"So you're not in love with her," Caydan stated.

"I didn't say that. I'm saying what is wrong with going slow?"

"Nothing. But you're in your forties. Life is slipping by my friend. If you want a little Patrick running around, you might want to think about settling down. And Gia is in her early thirties. Women start wanting children around that time. Even women who have careers."

Roger rolled his eyes. "I never would've believed it."

"What?"

"That meeting her parents was easier than sitting with you. All her father asked me for was to bring him snacks."

Caydan nodded. "Right. Translate that into come back so we can have a man-to-man talk. Roger, I've known you a long time. If this is the first woman you ever cared enough about to bring around to meet me, never mind meet her parents, just accept it. She's the one."

He didn't need Caydan to tell him that. He pretty much had deduced that the moment he laid eyes on her. She was the woman he'd take home to his parents, if they were still alive. "I'll give you that one, Caydan. There isn't anyone like her. There's a lot going on right now. She has a new job to deal with, and she's caring for her elderly parents. But I'm not going anywhere. Looks like Boston will be stuck with me a little longer."

"Just don't fuck it up in the meantime, because I'll never hear the end of it from Allyson," Caydan teased. "Remember, they all talk and stick together."

"Yeah. You're really selling me on that marriage stuff." Roger snorted. "Good thing you're not in sales. You suck at it."

"Yeah, but Allyson loves my sorry ass anyway." Then Caydan got up and said, "I'm heading out."

"To do what?"

"Golf, because I don't think either of those ladies will be back anytime soon. Want to join me?"

"Sure. It's been a long time since I've kicked your ass."

Caydan shrugged. "And I don't think today is going to change that."

As they walked out the hotel Roger felt like a weight had been lifted from his shoulders. He'd cleared the air with his best friend and finally admitted to himself how he felt about Gia. He loved her. Now all he needed to do was find the right time to tell her.

She's so good at research, she's probably already figured that out too.

CHAPTER 13

Roger had no intention of listening to what Caydan had to say. Marriage might be good for some, but for him, he wasn't sure. He had so much baggage he'd been avoiding. How was it fair to bring that into a relationship? It wasn't just the loss of the other agents that haunted him, but he never talked to anyone, professional or not, about losing his parents so young.

Roger had the ability, even at a young age, to hide his pain from the world. He didn't want that with Gia. If he wasn't willing to be open and honest with her, how could he expect it from her?

He drove around the block for the third time. It was pathetic. He was acting like some teenage boy who was about to tell a girl he liked her. Roger knew he was making this more awkward than it needed to be. So he pulled over to the first available spot and walked a block to her apartment.

Roger hadn't called Gia to see if she was home. For all he knew, she was out with one of the Henderson ladies, or back home checking on Andrew. *Stop trying to come up with excuses. Just go and fucking knock.*

As he opened the main entrance door he heard her voice calling from behind him. "Looking for me?"

He spun around to be greeted by her bright smile. "I was in the neighborhood and thought I'd stop by and say hello."

"Hello," she said, standing there.

This is where you invite me up. "How's your father doing?"

"He's good."

"Great." What was wrong with him? They'd spoken plenty of times; hell, they'd had amazing mind blowing sex, and now he couldn't think of what to say?

"Roger is everything okay?" Gia asked.

"Yes, why?"

"I don't know. Maybe it's because you're holding a bouquet of flowers, but not giving them to me. Unless they're for some other woman," she teased.

Fuck! This wasn't going as smoothly as he'd thought. He handed her the multi colored roses. It was crazy, but the woman at the florist shop had been telling him what each color meant. When he thought of Gia, she filled each one, so he did a bouquet filled with all the colors. After he purchased them, all he could think was when did that mushy romantic guy show up?

"They're beautiful. Thank you. Would you like to come up?

He nodded and followed her upstairs. When the door closed behind them, he watched as she put the roses in a vase. It gave him time to gather his thoughts. He was there to tell her he loved her. But he couldn't just blurt that out. She deserved something so fucking romantic that she'd never forget it. The flowers had felt like enough. *Had. Not so much now.*

Roger should take her out for a nice dinner. Hire someone

to come and play the violin to set the mood. And afterward, he could profess his undying love.

None of that was him. She either wanted the real Roger Patrick or she didn't. He'd learned a long time ago, you couldn't change a person. Thankfully he loved her just the way she was. Of course, in his eyes, she was perfect.

"Are you going to stand there all afternoon or would you like to sit?" Gia asked.

"Sorry. I have a lot on my mind," he said as he took a seat on the couch.

"So I noticed." He cocked a brow and she continued. "You drove past my apartment building three times. I was about to call and ask if you forgot which one was mine."

"You saw me?" She nodded as she joined him on the couch.

Well that's embarrassing. "I wasn't sure you were home."

"A phone call usually gets that answer quickly. Would you care to tell me what's really going on?"

"I wanted to see you. We haven't had a lot of alone time lately."

She smiled. "You're right. I'm working like crazy with your friends on the reunion. Which, by the way, I've been told to tell you, you're going one way or another. I think they mean it too."

He was serious when he said, "I'm not going unless it's with you."

"Roger Patrick, are you officially asking me out?"

Grinning he replied, "I guess I've done things backward, but yes, I'm asking you out."

"I'd love to go with you."

Roger pulled her to sit upon his lap. His mind was racing. She'd love to go with him, but love him might be a different story. There was only one way to find out that answer.

"Gia, I didn't come here to talk about the reunion. I came here to talk about . . . us." She didn't say anything, only listened. His hopes that she'd make it easy on him and wrap her arms around his neck telling him she loved him didn't happen. *She's going to make me earn this.*

"You're right. I kept driving past your place trying to figure out what to say. Damn it. I had even stopped at the store and picked out about five cards that seemed to say what I wanted. They may have been perfect, but they weren't mine. Hell, Gia, I know there are rules to how this is done, but I don't know any of them."

Gia put her hand on his cheek and asked, "Roger, some things don't have a rule book. You just need to follow your heart."

He covered her hand with his. "Heart? Gia, that's what I've been doing since the moment I saw you. No matter what I told myself, my heart continued to lead me back to you. I've tried to rationalize or use some sort of logic to figure this out. I can't explain it."

"Some things can't be explained, only felt," Gia said softly.

He nodded. "My rules of engagement that I utilize with every other aspect of my life, doesn't apply here. Being with you is like giving oxygen to someone who couldn't breathe. Everything instantly became better, easier. What I feel for you Gia . . . is more than I thought I was capable of. They are the simplest words that many utter all the time, but I have never spoken them before, until now. I love you, Gia." He saw her green eyes glisten, and she blinked back her tears. He fought kissing them away. Roger needed her to know what she meant to him. "Gia, I love you more than three words can express and more than I can show you in a lifetime. But all I know is I want to spend my life trying."

"Oh, Roger, I love you too. And you make me feel loved. When you showed up at the hospital and encouraged me, you showed that love. And when you went with me to my parents, I felt your love." A tear rolled down her cheek and he brushed it away. "And if you never told me, I'd have still known because you have stolen my heart. And I don't want it back."

He kissed her lightly. "I promise I'll take good care of it."

"You better, Roger"—she looked directly into his eyes —"because my heart is fragile and it's overflowing with love for you."

Roger's worries and concerns from before disappeared. He told her, but even greater, she felt the same. He claimed her lips and muttered *I love you* as he did. The words were said, now he wanted, no needed, to show her.

Her cell phone rang, and he pulled back briefly. "Do you need to get that?"

She nodded. "I'm sorry."

Gia slipped off his lap and instantly he wanted her back. When she returned he could see the desire that was there a moment ago was gone.

"Is everything okay?"

"Yes. It was my mother reminding me my father has his follow-up with the cardiologist today. I'm supposed to go with them."

Roger got up, walked over, and pulled her into his arms. "I hope we have time for one more kiss before we go."

"We?" Gia asked.

He nodded. "Told you, Gia. A lifetime of showing you."

"What have I done to deserve you?" she asked.

Roger teased, "Maybe it was those wild youthful years of yours."

Gia slapped his chest lightly. "I'll show you wild."

He winked. "Maybe tonight when we return. Now how

about that kiss?" He claimed her lips again, but this time it was different. It was a promise of what was to come.

As they parted and walked out the door Gia teased, "You know what this means, don't you?"

That I'm the luckiest man on the planet? "No, tell me."

"Now I have to stop by the bakery."

"Why?"

"Because every time my father asks about you, he also asks what you're bringing next time."

Roger laughed. "I think chocolate cream pie."

"I think you're going to get a lecture from the doctor today."

"Okay. I promise, you're the sweetest thing I'll bring with me."

She turned to him and said, "That's so corny it's cute."

He kissed her briefly again and added, "And true. I love you, Gia."

"I love you too, Roger."

Three words he knew he'd never grow tired of hearing her say. "So, scone again, I take it?"

She laughed. "How about a fruit salad?"

Roger grumbled. "So much for your father liking me."

"True, but my mother will appreciate you even more, and I love you. What more can you want?"

Absolutely nothing.

EPILOGUE

Gia looked all around and couldn't believe the Hendersons actually seemed to be having fun. It's what she envisioned as they had gathered to plan.

"You did an amazing job," Allyson said as she approached with two glasses of raspberry iced tea.

"We got lucky. It was a beautiful day. What I can't understand is how all these children are still running around. I'm exhausted just watching them." Even though none of the children where hers, she had put together some fun activities to keep them all busy. It had been nice to talk to her mother about it and get advice. She told Gia that whatever you plan, make it hands-on. No electronics either. "I have to give my mother credit too. The water balloons were a big hit."

"Oh they were a hit all right. I'm not going to forget the look on Dean's face when they ambushed him."

"That's what you get when you turn your back. Did his cell phone survive?" Gia asked. Since she was the little instigator on that, she would've felt bad if it had been ruined.

"I'm not sure, but Tessa said it was one way to get him to

follow the rules. If you notice, none of them are on their phones any longer." Allyson whispered. "Not even mine."

Tessa joined them. "Did I hear my name?"

"You did," Allyson admitted.

"Please tell me it was good."

Gia laughed. "We were thinking you might want to take home the extra water balloons."

Tessa grinned. "No way." Then she pointed to a super soaker water gun that was left on the ground. "Now that is something that temps me."

"Really? I thought you could sneak up on him better with a balloon." Allyson said.

"Yes, but if I miss, I'm done. At least this way I'm sure to get him eventually." Tessa laughed. "I can't tell you how much I have missed backyard barbecues. It reminds me of home."

"You're not from the city either?" Gia asked.

"Nope. I was raised in a small town, much like yourself. But Boston will always hold a special place in my heart."

Gia didn't need to ask why. The sparkling in Tessa's eyes when she looked at Dean said it all. If one didn't know, you'd think they were newlyweds.

Zoey and Morgan walked over and joined them. "Are you ladies thinking what we are?" They shrugged. "We all need to think about buying homes with bigger yards. Brunch is great, but this is . . . relaxing." They watched as Alex and Bennett chased after a few of the kids. "Well, for us at least. I honestly don't think I've ever seen my brothers behave like this." Then Zoey became very serious. "You have no idea what a gift you have given all of us. We never were allowed any of this growing up. God if something spilled or we came home dirty from playing at school, our father would have a fit. All we ever wanted was to be normal. It's been a long road, but I think we are finally there."

Gia looked at the mass amount of people and thought how small her family was in comparison. This was just the siblings, their children, and then a bunch of grandmothers she asked about. Allyson had tried explaining how James had eight children: six boys and two girls and each one of them had a different mother. Most of them where attending the reunion as well. It was beautiful that none seemed favored over the other.

"I didn't do much of anything. Just tossed a few ideas around. The real magic is in all the people who showed up," Gia said.

"I guess it's lucky we don't have any extended family, otherwise this might get really big really fast."

Yeah. About that. Gia kept her mouth shut. They were all happy, and that's all that mattered.

As they all stood watching the others play, Alex stepped to the left when he should've stepped to the right. Instantly a bunch of the boys tackled him to the ground. Once they knew no one was hurt, the ladies burst out laughing.

Gia realized it wasn't the road you were on in life as much as where it leads you. From what she learned, she knew their journeys were totally different, yet here they all were, blended into one huge happy family.

Gia counted this as a blessing, to be here and witness all of it. She might not be part of the family, yet they welcomed and included her and Roger as though they were.

Brice walked over and said, "Should I be worried that you're all plotting against me?"

"Why would you think such a thing?" Tessa asked.

"Because you all look way too happy. And with you ladies, that usually means trouble."

Zoey snickered. "We would never do such a thing. At least not without all the others. Remember brother dear. If one of you goes down, you all go down."

Morgan said, "Talk about going down, look at Shaun, Logan, and Roger trying to master the bicycle built for three. I probably should have my son, Tyler, go and show them how to do it before they break the thing." As soon as she said it, the bike went one way, then the other until it tipped all the way over. "Called it," she said as she walked away.

Brice said, "Someone once told me having kids keeps you young, but I learned with my first one, playing like they do makes it hard to walk the next day."

"Brice, don't become an old man before your time. You have a least another good year or two in you," Zoey teased. Then she said, "Guess it's my turn." She headed toward one of the little girls who was crying while holding her knee. "Looks like it's Band-Aid time."

"I should probably go and rustle mine up too. That's if I can get them to stop playing long enough to eat," Tessa said.

"You round them up, and I'll help serve," Allyson offered.

Before she knew it she was standing alone with Brice. She'd never had a direct conversation with him. He seemed so . . . unapproachable. Something told her he hadn't stayed to take in the scenery. He wanted to talk. She looked around, hoping Roger would notice and come join them. But he was too busy manning the grill with Caydan.

So small talk it is. "I can't believe how fast time goes by. Just a month ago you were counting the minutes till your baby would make her debut."

"Things do change quickly. You seemed to have settled in nicely in your new job."

"I'm still in the learning curve. But then again, I have a

feeling this position wasn't defined until I came aboard." She knew Roger had something to do with that. "It seems very much in line with what Roger has been encouraging me to do."

"How convenient."

Isn't it?

"I wanted to thank you for not sharing what you learned with anyone else. My family is the most important thing to me. You're loyalty is appreciated," Brice said.

"I gave my word to Roger I wouldn't say anything." Brice cocked a brow as though her point had been made. Her loyalty wasn't to him, it was to Roger. "But I'm very fond of your family as well. I wouldn't let anyone hurt them if I could prevent it. Brice, I do have my concerns though."

"What are they?" he asked.

"If I was able to find this information, don't you think someone else could too?"

"They would need to be looking. We have spent years since my father's death looking for what was going to hit us next. Do I think this will stay quiet forever? No. But I hope it waits long enough for us to enjoy this. We need a hell of a lot more of it."

Gia didn't know all of what their past had been. She didn't want to either. One secret was enough for her. "Then why don't you go and enjoy it? Monday comes fast enough, and we'll all be back to the grind."

Brice chuckled. "Funny, that's usually my line. Looks like Roger is abandoning Caydan so I better go help out before those burgers burn."

Gia wasn't alone very long before Roger joined her. "I never thought I'd get you alone."

"I was thinking the same thing. How did you escape cooking detail?"

He pulled her into his arms and said, "Simple, Brice was here, and I told Caydan you needed saving."

She looked up at him and said, "At a family party? What did you think he was going to do? Besides, I have a feeling his bark is much worse than his bite."

Roger laughed. "Oh he really does have you fooled."

Not in the least. I just know better than to push his buttons. Roger might be a good judge of character, but she wasn't so bad herself. "If he is as bad as he pretends to be, I don't think Lena would be married to him."

"They say love is blind," Roger teased.

Gia shook her head. "No. I think love is understanding and forgiveness and acceptance and sometimes"—she gave him a playful wink—"tolerance too."

Roger looked shocked. "What did I do?"

"Where would you like me to start?" she asked.

Softly Roger asked, "I guess with what I did wrong."

Gia smiled. "That's a mighty . . . short list."

He cocked his brow. "Then let's get that one out of the way."

"You forgot to bring me one of those burgers."

Roger laughed. "That's easily rectified. Would you like me to go now?"

"Don't you dare. I finally have some time with you." She had been so busy meeting the entire Henderson clan she'd barely had a moment to stop.

"Then what do you say we take a walk?" Roger asked.

She grinned and ran her fingers up his chest. "I have a better idea. What do you say we go home?"

Roger bent down and scooped her up into his arms. "I know this private beach that has the most amazing view of the stars."

"Who needs a shooting star when I already have everything I want in you?"

He looked down at her. "Gia, have I told you today how much I love you?"

He had several times already, but she'd never grow tired of it. "I'm not sure, maybe if you say it again, and this time with a kiss."

Roger said, "If I do that, we're leaving without saying goodbye. You might hear about it from the ladies tomorrow."

She knew he wasn't joking, and really, that was okay with her. Wrapping her arms around his neck Gia said, "I'm willing to risk it if you are."

Roger tightened his grip and headed to the car. Today might have been wonderful, but she knew tonight was going to be fantastic.

The End

Not ready to say goodbye to the Hendersons? Did you want to know more about the Lawson family, the Hendersons long lost cousins? Then get ready, because it all unravels in The Blank Check Series.

Book 1 The Billionaire's Rival Pre-Order Today
Releasing Date: July 20, 2019

ALSO BY JEANNETTE WINTERS

Barrington Billionaires Series:

Book 1: One White Lie (FREE!)

Book 2: Table For Two

Book 3: You & Me Make Three

Book 4: Virgin For The Fourth Time

Book 5: His For Five Nights

Book 5.5: New Beginning Holiday Novella

Book 6: After Six

Book 7: Seven Guilty Pleasures

Book 7.5: At the Sight of Holly

Book 8: Eight Reasons Why

Book 9: Nine Rules of Engagement

One White Lie

Brice Henderson traded everything for power and success. His company was closing a deal that would cement his spot at the top. The last thing he needed was a distraction from the past.

Lena Razzi had spent years trying to forget Brice Henderson. When offered the opportunity of a lifetime, would she take the risk even if the price would be another broken heart?

Do you love reading from this world? Continue with Always Mine from my sister, Ruth Cardello, Her series will mirror my time line. It isn't necessary to read hers to enjoy mine, but it sure will enhance the fun!

****

Betting on You Series:

Book 1: The Billionaire's Secret (FREE!)

Book 2: The Billionaire's Masquerade

Book 3: The Billionaire's Longshot

Book 4: The Billionaire's Jackpot

Book 5: All Bets Off

Book 6: A Rose For The Billionaire

Book 7: The Billionaire's Treat Novella

The Billionaire's Secret

Betting on You Series

Billionaire Jon Vinchi is a man with one passion: work. His friends decide to shake him up by entering him as a prize at a charity event.

Accountant Lizette Burke is dressed to the nines and covering for her boss at a charity event. She's hoping to land a donor for the struggling non-profit agency that employs her.

She never expected to win a date with a billionaire.

He never thought one night could turn his life upside down.

One lie stands between them and their happily ever after. Too bad it's a big one!

****

Southern Desires Series:

Book 1: Southern Spice (FREE!)

Book 2: Southern Exposure

Book 3: Southern Delight

Book 4: Southern Regions

Book 5: Southern Charm

Book 6: Southern Sass

Novella: Southern Hearts

Southern Spice

Derrick Nash knows the pain of loss. But is he seeking justice or revenge? He doesn't care as long as someone pays the price.

It is Casey Collin's duty at FEMA to help those in need when a natural disaster strikes. After a tornado hits Honeywell, she finds there are more problems than just storm damage. Will she follow company procedures or her heart?

Can Derrick move forward without the answers he's been searching for? Can Casey teach him how to trust again? Or will she need to face the fact that not every story has a happy ending?

****

Turchetta's Promise Series:

Book 1: For Honor (FREE!)

Book 2: For Hope

Book 3: For Justice

Book 4: For Truth

Book 5: For Passion

Book 6: For Love

Book 7: For Keeps

For Honor

Looking for a new Romantic Intrigue? Then you will love the Turchetta's. You met them in both the Betting On You Series as well as Barrington Billionaires Series. Now it is time for an up close look into their lives.

Rafe Turchetta may have retired from the Air Force, but his life was still dedicated to fighting the injustice of the world. There was one offense that went so wrong, and it will haunt him, as it continues to destroy him on the inside.

Deanna Glenn was being tortured by a tragedy, one that she couldn't share with anyone. Time was running out and she needed the lies to cease before she started to believe them herself.

Healing meant returning to where it all went horribly wrong years ago. For Deanna she needed to take on a new identity. For Rafe, that meant doing whatever he needed to in order to get her to speak the truth.

When danger rears its ugly head will Rafe follow his heart and protect Deanna even if it means never learning the truth? Or will Deanna sacrifice her happiness and expose it all?

****

Books by Ruth Cardello

ruthcardello.com

Books by Danielle Stewart

authordaniellestewart.com

Do you like sweet romance? You might enjoy Lena Lane

www.lenalanenovels.com

BY JEANNETTE WINTERS & LENA LANE

Muse and Mayhem Series

Book 1: The Write Appeal

Book 2: The Write Bride

Book 3: The Write Connection(2019)

Made in the USA
San Bernardino, CA
25 May 2019